IN H(BOUND

Brides By Chance
Regency Adventures
Book One

Elizabeth Bailey

SAPERE
BOOKS

IN HONOUR
BOUND

Published by Sapere Books.

20 Windermere Drive, Leeds, England, LS17 7UZ,
United Kingdom

saperebooks.com

ISBN: 978-1-913028-93-0

Chapter One

Now that the moment was almost upon her, Isolde's spirits drooped. A shiver shook her, not entirely attributable to the biting cold pervading the hired chaise.

"He'll hate me."

Mrs Quick clicked her tongue. "Now don't be putting the cart before the horse, me dearie. It's certain sure this de Baudresey fellow was fond enough of your poor papa, for the captain told you so."

"Yes, but that won't make him fond of me," Isolde argued.

"It won't signify. Many's the time I've heard him say as you'd be safe as houses with the gentleman."

"I won't be if he hates me."

"Why should he so?"

"You know very well why, Madge. Because I'm not a proper young lady and I don't want to be."

Mrs Quick sighed. "Then you'll be after learning how. Besides, you've nowhere else to go, and that's a fact."

This blunt reiteration of her dismal state did nothing to inspire Miss Cavanagh with confidence. Buoyed at first by the prospect of the adventure in travelling across the Channel to England, and in the knowledge of her future having been secured by Papa's foresight, it was not long before doubt set in. The journey seemed interminable, and the ship lurched so badly that Isolde's stomach threatened to regurgitate its contents. She remained on deck despite the inclement December wind, watching as the coastline gradually appeared, with all too much leisure to reflect upon her possible reception.

What if this Thomas de Baudresey repudiated her? Despite Papa's assurance, it was conceivable he might resent the intrusion into his household of a young girl with little knowledge of the customs obtaining amongst the gentry of England. Not that she wanted to know them. She would have to wear skirts all the time and curtsy. And there would be no danger of encountering an enemy soldier, so she'd have no use for her pistols or Papa's sword, carefully wrapped in the bottom of her trunk. Such skills as she possessed would go to waste. Who would want her to kill a rabbit or chicken, let alone skin and disembowel it ready for the pot?

The more she thought about it, the bleaker her prospects seemed. Already she missed the camaraderie of the camp, the cheery greetings from Papa's men and the dependable assistance of the other women who followed the drum. She could hardly bear the thought of Christmas without the merry, if ungainly, dancing to Sergeant Randall's fiddle, the competitions and raucous encouragement of the crowd as the champions wrestled for a prize, the smell of roasting chestnuts and succulent pig, the flowing ale and wine and, most poignant of all, Papa's infectious laughter.

There was no going back. She must make the best of it and learn a new way of life. No doubt the celebrations would be different, more staid and far less enjoyable.

A little of her optimism revived as the ship approached Langer Point and turned into the estuary. She had come here once before, when her mother died and Papa had come to fetch her, taking time to visit his friend before they sailed. Isolde was only nine at the time, and the memory of Colonel Sir Thomas de Baudresey was vague. But the instant she set eyes on the dark walls of Langer Fort, a sense of déjà vu attacked her.

Perhaps it would not be so bad. She was not altogether a stranger to the family. She had met the wife, though she could remember nothing about her. Her father had spoken with affection of his friend and mentor, who had been his colonel when Desmond Cavanagh was a mere lieutenant. He had told his daughter she would meet with nothing but kindness.

As the vessel sailed into Harwich harbour, Isolde managed to hold on to belief. It lasted through the meal at The Duke's Head, and the business of hiring the chaise. But the final leg proved her undoing. The closer they came to Bawdsey Grange, the more despondent she became.

By the time the carriage took a turn through a pair of open wrought-iron gates and built up speed again as the horses dragged the vehicle down a long drive, Isolde's heart was thrumming unevenly and her mouth felt dry. She clutched the reticule lying in her lap, feeling the stiff paper folded within that was all the passport she owned to have undertaken this journey.

She felt Madge's hand squeeze her arm.

"Courage now, me dearie. It'll be well, you'll see."

Isolde's lip trembled and her eyes pricked. "I wish you were staying with me, Madge."

"Well now, you know I can't do that, Izzy, my pet. I've no claim on your people here, and my family are waiting on me besides."

"They're not my people." Isolde eyed the matron's profile, unclear in the dim interior. "I could come with you to Ireland. Or at least as far as Cheshire. We could hunt out Mama's family. They could take me. They ought to take me."

"Now you know that's not possible, Izzy. Your papa told me they wouldn't want to know you, not after the way your mama ran off with him."

7

The carriage was slowing. Isolde made one last effort to avert her fate, speaking fast and low. "I could live with you, Madge, couldn't I? I'd work. I wouldn't be a burden. You know what I can do; you've known me long enough."

"I have, and I know it wouldn't be right. Will you be after coming down in the world? I'm not of your class. No, it won't do, even could I offer it. As it is, I'll be a beggar myself."

Isolde said no more. It was unfair to plague Madge. She had stayed far longer than her time only to take care of Isolde and bring her safe home. She'd have been long gone, if Captain Cavanagh had not begged her to stay and paid her way so she might chaperon his daughter, who was growing too fast to be permitted to roam alone among a company of soldiers. At least, that was the way it had started out, before Madge and Papa...

The door opened, and the guard was revealed behind it.

"This is the place, miss. Shall I help you down?"

He let down the steps, and offered a hand to assist Isolde to alight. She would have preferred to jump down without assistance, but she supposed she had best start behaving as a young lady should. She took the hand and stepped out, her eyes rising to take in the façade of Bawdsey Grange.

It rose above a set of wide stone stairs, with a pillared portico leading to a heavy front door. The house looked to be more sprawling than contained, rising only a couple of stories and spreading away to either side. Isolde breathed a little more easily. She had retained only a vague picture of a large, dark building, but although grey, the Grange was not the imposing mansion she had been imagining.

As she trod up the steps, she half expected the front door to fly open, disgorging a flood of servants. It remained closed and uninviting and she was relieved that Madge was at her side.

The coach was staying for her, but she had promised to see her charge into the care of the de Baudresey family before taking leave.

Isolde regarded the unresponsive door with a resurgence of the apprehension that had damped down with the business of exiting the coach and directing the guard to extract her luggage from the boot.

"I suppose I better knock."

Taking matters into her own hands, Madge stepped up to a lever to one side and gave it a tug, sending a bell pealing within.

The pitter-pat of her heartbeat increased as Isolde waited. It seemed an age before the door opened. A liveried footman appeared in the aperture. He directed an enquiring stare upon them, casting a look towards the coach.

The dance in Isolde's pulses abated, giving rise to irritation.

"Pray do not stare at me in that horrid fashion as if I was a slug on a cabbage. I am here to see Sir Thomas de Baudresey."

The footman's eyes widened, and his stare became even more austere. "If you mean Lord Alderton, miss —"

"Lord Alderton? No, I mean Colonel Sir Thomas de Baudresey. This is his house, is it not?"

The footman's brows drew together. "Perhaps you are not aware, miss, that Sir Thomas was granted a barony a matter of three or four years ago. He took the title of Lord Alderton."

It was Isolde's turn to stare. She glanced at Madge Quick, who met her eyes and grimaced, shrugging.

"My father could not have known." Isolde drew breath. "Well, it makes no odds if he is now a lord. He is the man I am here to see."

The footman's regard became pitying. "Then I fear you have made a wasted journey, miss. Lord Alderton has been dead these two years."

A sense of unreality invaded Isolde's mind. This could not be happening. If Sir Thomas — or Lord Alderton — had died, then she had no guardian at all. No guardian, no shelter and no future. Without thought, she spoke her mind aloud.

"Heavens, what am I to do now?"

Something of her dismay must have communicated to the footman, for he unbent a trifle.

"Perhaps you could state your business to the present Lord Alderton, miss?"

"The present Lord Alderton?"

"Richard de Baudresey, miss. Sir Thomas's son."

"I didn't know he had a son."

"It's not all you didn't know," murmured Madge.

Evidently noting how Isolde was too disconcerted to know what to do, she took a hand, addressing the footman in a high-handed fashion.

"Will you go and tell his lordship that Miss Cavanagh desires speech with him. And let us in, man! Will you be after leaving a lady on the doorstep? There must be room in a house this size for her to wait in comfort."

The footman looked taken aback, but he stood aside, gesturing for them to enter.

Madge hesitated on the doorstep.

"I've to see my charge safely received before I go, and I can see that may take a while. While you're fetching the trunk and portmanteau, would you tell the coachman where he may go to rest the horses and bait?"

"Certainly, madam."

The tone was repressive, but the footman slipped down the steps for a word with the coachman and guard, in which time Isolde stepped onto a chequered floor and took a moment to look around while she waited for the man's return.

A wide wooden staircase dominated the hall, leading up to a landing and branching off left and right to a gallery above. Doors led off either side, and Isolde glimpsed a green baize door at the back and the dark of a corridor behind the stairs. Two massive paintings of hunting scenes adorned panelled walls, and the excess of dark wood made the place dim in the dull winter afternoon. Candles were already alight in the wall sconces and a flaming candelabrum sat on a heavy oak table in a recess to one side.

The silence was oppressive, the shadows disquieting. Isolde's spirits plummeted.

Chapter Two

The faint tick of the library clock began to irritate, cutting into Richard's concentration. His pen paused, hovering over the paper on the desk. His writing, neat and precise as ever, covered more than half the page already and the words expressed but a tithe of what he needed to say.

With a sigh, he shifted the pen away from the sheet, careful to make no blots, and set it down in its cradle on the standish. Sinking back, he allowed his cramped muscles to relax against the leather-covered seat, and glanced at the clock above the mantel.

Past three already? He'd meant to have this business off his chest today, but time was pressing and he had to visit Mama before dinner.

He had known the letter was going to be difficult to write. He'd already ruined three sheets with earlier efforts, now shrivelled to ashes in the fire. He was still unsure if the present one would suffice. His lawyer had warned him to take care what he said, be wary just what he revealed. If he was to come out of this unscathed, Richard could not afford to botch it.

He greeted a knock at the door as a welcome interruption.

"Come."

The door opened and Richard recognised the stately figure of his butler.

"Oh, it's you, Topham. What is it?"

The man approached the desk with his customary measured tread, a hint of trouble in his usually urbane countenance under the domed head, which these days sported very little hair.

Richard's heart sank. What now? Hadn't he enough on his plate?

"A young lady is asking for you, my lord."

"What young lady?"

"A Miss Cavanagh, my lord."

Richard frowned in an effort of memory. "I don't know anyone of that name."

"No, my lord, but I venture to think the name was well known to your honoured father."

"Oh?"

"Yes, my lord. Fortunately, James had the sense to apprise me of the young lady's arrival."

Vague recollection stirred in Richard's mind. "I thought I heard a carriage. Who is this Miss Cavanagh and what does she want with me?"

The butler gave his gentle cough, a sign that he had already vetted the lady's credentials and found them acceptable. "That I cannot take it upon myself to say, my lord, for the young lady asked for your lordship's late father. According to James, she was unaware of his having acquired the title, or of his demise. I conceived it to be my duty to question the young lady myself."

"And clearly decided that I ought to see her. Has she some claim upon me?"

"I could not say, my lord. But when I learned the young lady's identity, it struck me that his late lordship would desire you to receive her."

Richard eyed him, suspicion building in his head. This could not be the result of an indiscretion of his father's, could it? Was he to be saddled with yet another embarrassment? "Well?"

Topham's features took on the austere expression he was wont to adopt whenever he considered Richard to have overstepped the mark. That was the worst of these retainers who had known one from birth. They took too many liberties, and one could neither snub them nor send them packing. And Topham was particularly prone to champion any suit of his father's.

"Captain Cavanagh, my lord, was a particular friend and protégé of his late lordship. I have often heard him speak of the man with affection."

Richard ignored the tone of reproof. "Was? Is the fellow dead then?"

"So I understand, my lord. Miss Cavanagh is here, as she explained to me, under Captain Cavanagh's direction."

Damnation, he was going to be saddled with some wench from his father's past! Why else should the wretched fellow send the girl here? He damped down the rising annoyance. "I suppose I must see her then. Where is she?"

On tenterhooks, Isolde knew not whether to be fearful or to give way to a strong desire to fall into hysterics. Her dismay had given way to a budding sense of ill-usage. Not only had she been parked in this bare, if neat, room, boasting little more than a couple of chairs and a small sofa, but she had been subjected to a catechism by an elderly individual whose austerity all but crushed her. Already she hated the place. And she was much inclined to resent the necessity to sue for mercy to this unknown son of Sir Thomas's.

Madge, who had occupied herself with examining what she could see of the grounds from the window which at least gave light into the room, had urged her to be calm.

"It's no manner of use putting yourself into a passion, Izzy. Wait until you see how the land lies."

But Isolde could see very well how it lay, and she wanted no part of it. How wretched that she'd been born a female, to be subject to the whim of strangers and obliged to behave in a fashion as dull as it was depressing.

Pacing a large rug from end to end and back again, she was caught unawares when the door opened. She stopped dead and turned her eyes towards the doorway, unconsciously affording the man who entered a perfect opportunity to take in her state of mind.

He did not appear to notice it, although a pair of keen eyes appraised Isolde as readily as she appraised him. She could not doubt his identity. Everything about him proclaimed the gentleman, and his air of ownership could not be mistaken.

Dark hair, lush and worn long so it rested on his collar, framed features more striking than handsome. Isolde received an impression of strength coupled with neatness, of both garb and motion. He moved with grace as he came towards her, and gave a small bow.

"Miss Cavanagh?"

For a moment she did not speak, daunted by the formality of his manner. But he was not forbidding. A faint sense of relief crept through her and she gave it voice without thought. "You haven't come to throw me out then?"

His brows lifted. "Should I do so?"

"Well, it's true I have no claim upon you. Indeed, I can't be sure your father would have welcomed me either, so why in the world should you?"

One corner of his mouth quirked. "You are very frank."

Isolde was conscious of a sliver of warmth in the cold of her isolation. "I've never learned discretion. Not in conversation, I mean. We had no use for it in the camp."

"You followed the drum?"

A mist formed in Isolde's vision and her voice sank. "It's all I've known. You won't find me of the least use in a drawing room, I warn you."

"Isolde, me dearie, will you be telling his lordship everything that must set him against you?" Madge was at her elbow, her gaze turned to the man. "You'll forgive her boldness, me lord, and I'll take leave to say she's a deal more capable than she'll give herself credit for."

Lord Alderton's brows drew together. "I beg your pardon, ma'am. You are?"

"Mrs Quick, me lord, and I've had charge of the girl these three years. I'll not pretend to the knack of making a lady of her, but she'll learn swift, you'll see."

"Madge!"

Her mentor turned to her. "It's truth, me dearie, and I'll not have his lordship think badly of you when there's no need." She turned again to the gentleman. "She's young yet, sir. It's sure I am as you'll make allowances."

Isolde could bear no more. "Oh, stop, Madge, you make me sound the veriest ninny!"

Lord Alderton intervened. "I thank you, Mrs Quick, but I must point out that I have as yet no inkling of what Miss Cavanagh expects me to do for her."

"Nothing! At least, I don't expect it. It's what Papa told me to do. And you are not your father, and not his friend, and I don't see why you should be obliged to house me, let alone be my guardian."

"Your guardian! Good God!"

Isolde's nerves shattered and an involuntary sob escaped.

Chapter Three

Quite as bewildered as astonished, Richard watched the matron hustle her charge away from him, muttering Lord knew what soothing words to calm her. The woman's role was unclear, for although her accent and style of speech suggested her station in life, both manner and dress precluded any idea of servitude. Indeed, the great-coat was of excellent cut and the bonnet boasted more feathers and ribbons than Miss Cavanagh's headgear.

His first sight of the girl had taken him aback. The face turned towards him had been ripe with distress and anger both, its features nevertheless striking, with creamy white skin sprinkled with freckles and expressive eyes that mirrored every passing thought. Richard thought he caught a glimpse of reddish hair under the bonnet. A tall creature, svelte under a close-fitting great-coat. But Lord above, so young!

Reminded of the girl's last words, he felt a resurgence of shock. What in the world had his erratic parent burdened him with this time?

"Miss Cavanagh!"

The girl turned from the window where she'd been standing with her back to him, flanked by the still-whispering duenna — if that was what she was.

"My butler spoke of a letter."

Consternation entered the misted eyes, though they were thankfully no longer seeping tears.

"Oh. Yes, I forgot."

"May I see it, if you please?"

She seized up a reticule that had been lying on one of the chairs and came towards him, tugging open the strings. She halted before him as she dug into its depths.

It struck Richard that she showed no sign of shyness, despite her evident dismay at her predicament. He took the letter she held out to him, meeting the apprehensive look in her eyes. "Thank you."

"It's to your father."

"So I understand."

He unfolded the sheet and swiftly read the letter, conscious throughout of the girl's anxious regard, which he found singularly disconcerting, inhibiting concentration.

From this cursory reading, he gathered that Captain Cavanagh had relied upon an age-old suggestion made by his wayward parent, typically vague, that in the event of his demise, his daughter would be welcome to seek succour at his home. Richard had no doubt whatsoever that this lightly-uttered notion had been taken in a more literal spirit than had been intended, moving the captain to name his friend as guardian to his only child.

His father would have laughed it off, Richard made no doubt of that. His generous spirit would have prompted him to pecuniary assistance, and perhaps he might have bestirred himself to help the girl find employment. But take her in and make himself her guardian? Richard could have laughed, were it not so tragic.

His gaze rose and he regarded the anxious face before him with pity, not unmixed with exasperation, which found instant expression.

"I take it you are quite alone in the world? You have no relatives?"

Miss Cavanagh's lips trembled a little and uncertainty entered the eyes. Green? Or tending more to hazel? Richard noted gold flecks within the colour.

"My mother's family will not own me. Papa did not wish me to go to them."

The sense of this penetrated Richard's abstraction. "Then you do have family. Why should you not make contact with them?"

Miss Cavanagh's fingers strangled her reticule and Richard's sense of compassion deepened.

"My mother ran away with Papa. He said they wanted nothing more to do with her. He said they wouldn't want me either."

"Either?"

"You don't want me. Your father wouldn't want me. Madge can't have me. Nobody wants me."

Richard could not deny it, but he entered a caveat, against his own belief. "You can't know that my father would not have wanted you. Nor, I may add, can you make such an assumption about me."

Indignation sparkled. "Yes, I can. I can see very well you don't wish me to be here. Well, I don't wish to be here either, but I had no choice. You can send me packing if you like. I don't care. I'll make my own way. I know how to look after myself."

Despite himself, Richard's lips twitched, and he had all to do not to burst out laughing. "From the little I've seen of you, Miss Cavanagh, I have no doubt you are very well able to look after yourself. However, you might find it a trifle awkward, with no home to go to and no money to speak of. Or am I wrong about that? Perhaps your father left you some provision?"

Miss Cavanagh regarded him with defiance clear in her face. "I've got all the guineas he had when he died, and the colonel gave me his last pay. As for a home, I've lived in nothing but billets and tents for years and made a home wherever we were. Besides, I can find work and they are bound to let me live there too."

He kept to himself the inevitable reflections set up in his mind as to the kind of life Miss Cavanagh was likely to find herself in if she was left without protection.

"I can see you have worked it all out, but perhaps it would be better if you were to remain here while we decide what is best to be done."

She did not soften, suspicion in her gaze. But was there a measure of relief?

He looked past her to the woman who accompanied her. "And you, Mrs Quick?"

She hurried forward. "You'll not be thinking you've to accommodate me as well, me lord. I'm off again without delay, for the coach is waiting for me."

This was unexpected, and decidedly unwelcome. What, was she here merely to dump the girl and run?

"I thought you said you had charge of Miss Cavanagh?"

"So I did, me lord, but I undertook only to see her safe into Sir Thomas's protection. I'm behind my time by three years already and I am expected."

"Madge only stayed after Sergeant Quick died to care for me," chimed in Miss Cavanagh, her chin coming up. "I'd go with her if I could, but she can't afford me and I don't want to be a burden to anyone."

The words came out in a rush, more than a touch of rebellion in the tone. Dismay crept into Richard's chest. Miss

Cavanagh was likely to prove a handful, especially without the woman Madge to curb her.

"May I request you to stay for a day or two at least, Mrs Quick? A short delay can make little difference, I must suppose."

The matron looked doubtful, Miss Cavanagh mulish. Richard ignored the latter, concentrating his attention on Mrs Quick. He hit a persuasive note.

"It will be hard for Miss Cavanagh to be pitched into an unknown milieu without the presence of someone with whom she is well acquainted."

From the corner of his eye, he noted the girl's sudden intent look. Had she no notion of anyone looking to her comfort?

"Well, I could spare a night," said Mrs Quick in a grudging fashion, "but I'll not be after staying to carry on where I left off, and so I warn you, me lord."

"No, indeed, I —"

"It's not as I'm not fond of Izzy, as I hope she knows, but I've a life of my own to lead and it's high time I went at it."

Miss Cavanagh did not appear to resent this blunt admission. She looked rather resigned, if a trifle glum.

Richard seized on the respite. "I thank you, Mrs Quick. Your support, if only for one night, will be welcome." He crossed to the bell-pull and tugged. "My housekeeper will see to your needs. No doubt you would both wish to put off your outer garments and repair the stains of travel."

He turned to find both women staring at him, Mrs Quick with approval not unmixed with suspicion, the girl with astonishment. He hid a smile and moved towards the door, but a stray thought stayed him and he turned back.

"Izzy?"

His puzzlement was evidently not lost on Miss Cavanagh. Her chin came up.

"Isolde."

A vague recollection came to him and he lifted the letter he still held, hunting through the words. "Oh yes, I see it. Isolde Mary Cavanagh." He glanced at the youthful face and back to the letter. It was dated several years back. Had she carefully preserved it all this time? There was no clue in the date. "How old are you, Isolde?"

His use of her name produced a sudden bright smile that lit her face and sent a cascade of unexpected warmth through Richard's chest.

"I am seventeen."

A sense of disorientation invaded Richard's mind. Seventeen and quite lovely. And the wretched child had become his responsibility.

The door opened to admit the footman. He had never been more glad of an interruption.

"Ah, James. Desire Mrs Pennyfather to come to this room. Immediately, if you please."

Chapter Four

"What in the world am I to do with the girl, Mama?"

Lady Alderton sighed, sinking back against the cushions propping her up where she lay on the chaise longue. Richard was relieved she was well enough to have left her bed today, for he would otherwise have been reluctant to burden her with the problem of Isolde Cavanagh. She was failing fast and ought not to be troubled, but the habit of consulting her was ingrained. Besides, she was unlikely to remain in ignorance of such an invasion, deep as she was in Pennyfather's confidence.

"You will naturally do what your conscience dictates, my dear Richard."

He was at once irritated. "I thank you, ma'am, that is singularly helpful."

A tiny choke of laughter escaped her and the worn features relaxed. "In this instance, dearest boy, I fear I cannot help you. Were I in health —" She broke off, biting her lip.

Richard did not take it up. Of all things, his mother hated to discuss the consequences of her prolonged illness. "What of this Captain Cavanagh? Did you know him?"

"I met him a time or two. A charming rogue, I thought him. One of these care-for-nobodies who attack life in a large-minded spirit and refuse to count the cost."

"Like my father, you mean."

The bitter note could not be suppressed, and Richard caught the look of reproach from his mother's grey eyes.

"Thomas was a good man, Richard. Misguided on occasion, I grant you, but he always meant well."

"I never doubted the sincerity of his intentions."

Which was true enough, if only his father had not pledged chunks of his inheritance in support of bizarre projects. Enough to endanger the prosperity of the estates. And now this orphaned girl must needs appear on his doorstep, claiming his father's guardianship, which was likely to make it impossible for him to repudiate her.

"What about the girl? Do you suppose my father really meant what the captain claims in that letter?"

Lady Alderton picked it up from where it was lying in her lap and read it again. "Oh, I expect he said something of the sort and I am sure he meant it at the time."

"Just so. He never thought it would come home to roost though, did he?"

A little smile of reminiscence curved his mother's mouth. "I very much doubt he remembered it at all."

Exasperation mounted into Richard's breast. That was precisely the point. His father's too-easy generosity had been apt to prompt him to promises impossible for his son to keep. It never seemed to occur to him that the individuals who sought the late Lord Alderton's investment in whatever crazy scheme they had dreamed up would actually come calling when the finance was needed.

"He never meant to leave you so encumbered, my dearest," came his mother's plaintive plea.

Richard let out a breath. "You need not tell me so."

No one could have anticipated that his father, the epitome of rude health, would succumb to the ravages of the fever that had swept the village. He had taken it from one of his tenants, fallen ill almost immediately and was dead within a matter of days. Richard knew his mother had never recovered from the blow, and was inclined to attribute the wretched wasting disease that was slowly killing her to the shock of her loss.

"Cavanagh brought the girl here once."

Richard snapped back to the current difficulty. "You mean you've met her?"

"Briefly, years ago. She was a skinny child. I vaguely recall a white and frightened little face and tangled red hair."

"Yes, that's her," Richard said instantly, the image of Isolde Cavanagh leaping into his mind. "Not tangled, but certainly white of face. And yes, a little afraid under the bravado, I believe."

"Bravado?"

A laugh escaped him. "She's a rebel, if I don't miss my guess. She informed me that she is perfectly well able to take care of herself and invited me to throw her out."

His mother's amusement lightened his mood.

"You won't do that, of course."

"Of course not. But as to taking up the mantle of her guardian, that is another matter altogether."

"What will you do then?"

"Make an effort to find these relatives on her mother's side. Cavanagh warned her not to apply to them since it appears his wife became estranged from her family after they eloped."

Lady Alderton was frowning. "What is her family?"

"That I have not yet discovered."

"And if they refuse to take her?"

Richard shifted his shoulders. "I'll cross that bridge when I come to it."

His mother smiled and held out the letter. "Well, if the worst comes to the worst, at least there is Alicia."

Sudden hope lit in Richard's chest. He had forgotten his sister, who was currently away, taking care of some domestic issue at the London house. He eyed his mother as he took the

25

letter, folding it in his habitual neat fashion and tucking it away into the inner pocket of his coat.

"Do you suppose Alicia would consent to take care of the girl?"

"Why not? She will not long have me on her hands, after all."

There could be no denying the truth of this, although Richard found it hard to contemplate an end he dreaded. Doctor Loader had warned him his mother was unlikely to see Christmas. Moreover, he was by no means convinced Alicia would regard the entrance into their lives of an undoubtedly pert young madam with any degree of complaisance. He foresaw a wearing argument.

Chapter Five

There was, Isolde was obliged to admit, a deal of pleasure to be had in lying in a feather bed, the sheets already warmed, the pillows soft, quilt snug about her body. She had meant to devote her mind to discovering a means of changing her situation, but instead found herself revelling in the unaccustomed luxury.

She had eaten in company with Madge in the small parlour they had first inhabited, back to which the housekeeper led them, saying that Lord Alderton thought they would prefer to dine privately on this occasion. Isolde was glad of it, by then feeling overawed by the size and style of the establishment in which she found herself. The house was large and rambling, the corridors many and bewildering. But the bedchamber assigned to her was cosy and warm, the bed so comfortable that, instead of bending her mind to her problems, Isolde fell swiftly into a dreamless sleep.

She woke refreshed and a little more hopeful. Although she had not again seen Lord Alderton yesterday, he had not so far shown any disposition to eject her from his home. After consigning her and Madge to the care of his housekeeper, he had vanished.

What he meant to do remained a mystery, but Isolde recalled his saying she might remain while a decision was made. It gave her a respite at least, time in which to consider what was best for her to do. But if Lord Alderton supposed he was going to determine her future, he was mightily mistaken.

She stretched luxuriously, wondering what time it was and whether she should get up. A faint light was creeping in through the closed shutters as well as the glow from a freshly-made fire. Someone had been in to make it up. How had she not heard them? Back in camp, there would be no fire until she made it up herself, and all too likely outside of a tent. A fire in her bedchamber was unheard of. Indeed, she'd had no bedchamber to call her own until Madge had joined them, invariably sleeping in an improvised apartment divided from Papa's bed by a curtain that travelled with them for the purpose.

But Madge had insisted upon her occupying separate quarters and Isolde had been banished to another small tent or a separate room in whatever billet they managed to acquire.

A knock at the door interrupted her ruminations, and was immediately followed by the entrance of a youthful maid, labouring under the weight of a huge metal can of hot water.

Instinct sent Isolde flying out of the bed. "Here, let me help with that." She made to grasp at the can, but the girl held it back, astonishment in her eyes. "It looks heavy," Isolde said.

"I'm used to it, miss. Mrs Pennyfather would have my guts for garters if I let you help, miss."

Isolde took a firm grasp of the can. "Then don't tell her."

The maid giggled, but she shook her head too. "I dursn't for my life, miss." She set the big can down on the floor. "You could bring your jug so I can fill it, if you like, miss."

Isolde went to the basin and ewer set on a commode in a corner of the room and brought the jug across, setting it down and holding it steady while the younger girl filled it with the steaming hot water.

"Thank you."

"You're welcome, miss." The maid lifted up the large can with apparent ease and went to the door. She turned there as she set her fingers upon the handle. "Ain't none in this house ever offered afore, miss. You won't take it amiss if I say as it won't do to be trying to help us servants. Mr Topham'd get all uppity and say as you weren't no lady, miss."

Isolde sighed, resisting the impulse to tell the girl she had no desire to be a lady, especially if it meant that she must watch others do things she was perfectly well able to do for herself. "Thank you for the warning. What's your name?"

"Becky, miss."

Isolde gave her a smile and was pleased to see the maid's face light up. She was little more than a child. "Well, Becky, I'm very glad to have made a friend in this house. I have a suspicion I'm going to need one."

Another giggle broke from the girl at this, and she hastily smothered it, dropped a curtsy, and left the room.

A little cheered, but with apprehension returning, Isolde began upon her ablutions. Hadn't she known how badly equipped she was to become a proper lady? Already she'd made a fool of herself. Even the maid knew better than she did what was expected of a female of her station.

She was already dressed when Madge came to fetch her.

"That Mrs Pennyfather is coming to take you to the breakfast parlour."

Isolde was quick to catch the emphasis. "Me? What about you?"

"I've had a tray in my room."

There was a spark in Madge's eye and Isolde eyed her with misgiving. "What's happened, Madge?"

Her erstwhile duenna shrugged. "Nothing to worry you, my pet, but I'll not be staying any longer."

"But Lord Alderton asked you to stay for a couple of days."

"So he did, but as I told him, I'm waited on and I can't be delaying. It's plain to see his lordship is after taking care of you, one way or another, so my duty's done and I can leave you with my conscience clear."

Isolde was not fooled. She had not been around the camp women for years without learning to recognise when offence was taken. Had something been said? Or hinted at? If so, she had a shrewd notion what it might be, but there was no speaking of that. She tried again. "Madge, you're upset, I know you are."

"Well, if I am, it's all the more reason to be taking myself off."

A toss of the head accompanied these words and Isolde recognised the flash of anger in Madge's eyes. She tensed, remembering quarrels that had erupted between this woman and Papa on occasion. She eyed the woman askance, and Madge caught the look.

"You've no need to look at me so, me dearie. It's no worse than I'd expect, folks being what they are."

Now Isolde was certain she understood. Never having openly discussed the matter, she could not mention it now. Madge must be allowed her dignity.

Instead, she threw her arms about her duenna's neck and hugged her, a tremulous note in her voice. "I don't care, Madge. You've been a mother to me. I understand you have to go, but I don't know how I'll go on without you."

The embrace was returned with fervour.

"You're a strong lass, Izzy, my pet. You'll do." She pulled back and her eyes were rueful. "I could never have stayed, you know that, don't you?"

The hurt stabbed. "They won't accept me any more than you, Madge. I'm not like them."

"But you were born to it, Izzy, and you'll be finding your feet in a while." She let out a reluctant laugh. "And if you ask me, that young lord won't be after dealing you short shrift. I'm thinking he's the dutiful kind. He'll stand buff."

A stealthy sound alerted him and Richard looked up from his plate in time to see the Cavanagh girl slip into the breakfast parlour to stand by the door, regarding him with a frowning stare. He rose.

"Good morning, Miss Cavanagh. I trust you slept well?" He nodded to the footman, who immediately set a chair for her. Richard waved her across. "Do sit down. James will serve you. What would you like?"

He watched her trip across the room, a wary look creeping into her face. Without the concealing hat and great-coat, she looked nervous and very young. He noted the bright hair, caught up at the back and curling into her neck, a few short tendrils escaping to lie against her cheek. Her features were pale, her eyes dilated.

As she came closer, Richard found himself gazing at those eyes, their indeterminate colouring again a puzzle.

The girl's head dropped as she took her seat, veiling them from his glance.

Richard sat down again. "Coffee?"

She looked up quickly and nodded. He signed to the footman, who upended her cup and poured the dark liquid. Her gaze followed the movements, but still she did not speak.

Richard tried again. "We have eggs, ham and beef. What is your choice?"

She looked at him and he caught the tremble in her lip. "Madge is leaving." The words were blurted out, a faint accusation in them.

Richard frowned. "Your duenna?"

"She isn't that. She never was."

Damnation! Hadn't he requested the woman to remain, if only briefly? He looked to the footman. "Send someone to fetch Mrs Quick here at once." James immediately left the room, and Richard infused reassurance into his tone. "She can't leave without my help, you know. The coachman couldn't wait."

Isolde looked startled. "They've gone?"

"I sent them away."

"Madge won't like it."

"When she wants to go, I'll send her in my own coach."

The girl's eyes narrowed. "She wants to go now. She's insulted."

Richard blinked. "She's what? Who insulted her?"

"You did," she accused. "Your housekeeper told us it was because you thought we'd rather eat alone, but that's not why, is it? Madge isn't quality and you don't want her to share your board."

The tone was low, but Richard could hear the anger vibrating within it. He took his time about his answer. The girl was shrewd, no doubt of that. "As a matter of fact, I expected her to come in with you this morning."

"Then it wasn't by your orders she had a tray in her room for breakfast?"

"Certainly not." He was prevented from saying more by the re-entrance of the footman.

"I've sent a maid for Mrs Quick, my lord."

He nodded and then gestured at Isolde's empty plate. "It won't serve any useful purpose to starve. What will you eat?"

She let out a little sigh and some of the belligerence faded. "Eggs, if you please."

Richard glanced at James, who was already picking up the requisite silver dish from the sideboard. He waited while Isolde was served, and then resumed his own meal. "You may give me a trifle more ham, James."

The man complied and Richard watched the young girl hesitate before picking up a fork. It flashed into his mind that she was unsure which utensil she should use. Was she really so ignorant of social customs?

Before he could pursue the thought, the door opened to admit the older female, who strode in with a bold step and came to rest at the other end of the table, radiating displeasure.

"You sent for me, me lord?"

Bent on disarming her, Richard smiled and gestured to the chair at his other side. "Good morning. Won't you take a cup of coffee, Mrs Quick?"

He noted Isolde's quick glance go from her chaperon to himself and back again. Puzzled by his tactics?

"You'll not be after inviting the likes of me to sit at your table."

Richard rose. "On the contrary. Please."

He gestured again, and the woman sniffed, her chin going up. Richard waited, refusing to look at Isolde, yet aware she was eyeing him.

Mrs Quick gave in, her shoulders dropping as she moved to take the indicated chair.

Isolde leaned a little across the table, whispering, "It wasn't his fault, Madge. He says he didn't order it."

In fact Richard had said nothing beyond suggesting the parlour meal last night. The only thought in his mind had been a wish to delay further discussion with the child until he'd had time to think about the situation. Pennyfather had taken it in a literal spirit. Or had she made a more accurate judgement of Mrs Quick's status than he had? He could determine that later. At this present, his sole desire was to keep the woman here until his sister should be home to lend Isolde countenance.

"I understand from Miss Cavanagh that you were planning to leave this morning."

The woman's fire flashed. "I am going, sir. You won't stop me."

"Madge, he sent away the coach. You can't go yet."

"Oh, can't I?" She turned an irate face on Richard. "Am I to take it you took it upon yourself to pay off the coach? I'd the hiring of it to take me to catch the stage from Harwich."

"I am aware of that."

"Then you'll be good enough to send me there in your own vehicle, or I'll know the reason why."

Richard played his ace. "But would you not be more comfortable travelling post?"

She was momentarily silenced. Richard caught Isolde staring, open-mouthed, and was obliged to bite down on a laugh.

Mrs Quick found her tongue. "All the way to Ireland? You've windmills in your head, me lord."

"At my expense, of course." He saw her eyes widen in shock, and added in tones of silk, "Assuming, of course, you are ready to oblige me by remaining for a space to chaperon Miss Cavanagh."

"That's bribery, is that." But the tone held grudging respect.

Richard laughed. "Just so, Mrs Quick. I will lose no sleep over it, for my reason is sufficient."

The woman's features hardened. "Aye, and so is mine." She shook her head. "I'll not be beholden. Nor I won't be held to ransom. I've done as I said I'd do, and I'll not stay to be slighted."

"No one will slight you, Mrs Quick. I must apologise if any in this household has received you with less respect than you deserve."

Unexpectedly, the matron let out a laugh. "Well, and we'll be saying nothing of deserts, if you please. But I won't remain, for all of that." Richard opened his mouth to speak, but the woman held up a hand. "Oh, I have your measure, me lord. But you'll not get your servants to pretend. I'd feel it every moment, and I'll not stay for it."

"Then will you stay for Isolde?" said Richard, trying one last desperate throw.

The girl interrupted before Mrs Quick could respond. "She won't. Madge owes me nothing. I told you before, she doesn't want the charge of me."

"No, and you know why, Izzy."

Despite himself, Richard was unable to keep the exasperation from his voice. "No one expects you to take charge of her. I am merely asking you to wait until my sister returns from London."

"Pray when might that be?"

"A few days at most. I'll write to her today."

Mrs Quick sighed. "It's no manner of use, me lord. Besides, from what I hear, there's another lady in the house."

"My mother is far too unwell to act as chaperon."

Mrs Quick rose from the chair. "I've nothing more to say, except to ask you to let me have your coach as far as Harwich. I'll take that much, seeing as you took it upon yourself to strand me here."

Pride kept Richard from further argument. It struck him that the woman's determination had been fixed yesterday, and she would not swerve from it. He told James to ring the bell, wondering what he was missing. The woman must have pressing reasons of her own for this inexplicable obstinacy. He recalled Isolde saying the woman did not want the charge of her. It occurred to him now to wonder why.

Chapter Six

The coach rumbled slowly down the drive and Isolde watched it out of sight, tightness gathering in her chest. The last link with her father, with the life she'd known, was disappearing along with Madge. Bereft, she struggled for the courage to hide the lonely despair, an echo of the grief she'd felt at her father's last farewell.

She'd stood with his company, dry-eyed and still, as the makeshift coffin was lowered into the ground, the sound of the bugle burning its message into her heart.

"Miss Cavanagh?"

She started, turning to find Lord Alderton at the top of the steps.

"You'll take cold. Come inside."

The tone was a command and Isolde obeyed, climbing the steps and walking swiftly past him, head lowered. She went through the front door the butler was holding open and came to a halt in the middle of the hall.

Where was she to go? What was she to do? She had no place here, and no one to help her find it.

"Come into the library."

Lord Alderton was at her side, a hand on her elbow, guiding her to the back of the hall behind the staircase and into a corridor with several doors leading off it. Isolde found herself in a huge room lined with bookshelves, bright from the light streaming in through massive windows, where cushioned seats sat in the alcoves. She vaguely took in the ample desk to one side, the set of globes and the big and clumsy library steps, and then the hand at her elbow persuaded her down into a deep chair to one side of a marbled fireplace, where the warmth from the grate pervaded the ice in her bosom.

She watched Lord Alderton take a seat in an identical chair set opposite and met his glance as he looked across.

"I'm sorry I could not persuade her to stay."

Isolde pushed her voice up through the fog. "I knew she wouldn't."

"Do you know why?"

The question penetrated her absorption. "She told you why."

"I'm not sure I believe her."

Isolde was swept with a new sensation, of apprehension mixed with a liberal dose of suspicion. "What do you mean?"

A faint smile crossed his features, softening them, and Isolde felt a stir of warmth and hope. "I had no intention of being obtuse. I suspect Mrs Quick had some other reason than she chose to reveal to me."

Wary now, Isolde eyed him. Had he divined the truth? He might hazard a guess. Mrs Pennyfather had not hesitated to show her suspicions. She hastened to deflect him. "What are you going to do with me?"

His look became enigmatic, but he held her eyes. "That, Isolde, is the question that is exercising my mind."

His use of her name sent an odd flitter down her veins, though Isolde could not have said why. She waited for what he might say next.

"Have you any notions of your own?"

That was unexpected. She drew a quick breath and let it out. "I told you in the first place. I don't know how to be a lady." She hesitated, but he did not speak, merely holding her with a gaze that told her nothing of his thoughts. "I can work. I told you that too."

His brows rose. "What did you have in mind?"

"I can cook and clean, wash clothes." He said nothing, and Isolde was emboldened to enumerate a few of her other skills. "I know it won't be needed in England, but I used to set up camp within the hour, and have the fire going and a meal in the pot in a trice. Rabbit, or a chicken if we could get one. I'm good with horses too."

"You ride?"

She did not miss the note of relief, and warmth stole into her cheeks. If he supposed there was at least one thing she did that didn't flout convention, he was sadly mistaken. "Yes, but I know I wouldn't be allowed to here."

"Why not? Ladies do in England, you know."

"Not astride."

His eyebrows shot up and Isolde collapsed with dejection.

"I knew you'd hate me. I told Madge."

To her surprise, and indeed dismay, he laughed. "My dear Miss Cavanagh, how should I hate you? I barely know you. A state of affairs I am trying to remedy." The softer look vanished. "Well, let us be a little more realistic, shall we? I appreciate that you have lived something of a gypsy life, but surely Mrs Quick must have taught you a little of what you need to know to take your place in society?"

Isolde shook a miserable head. "Nothing. She doesn't know any more than I do."

"But there must have been other ladies in the camp."

He sounded incredulous and Isolde could not help feeling resentful. Was it her fault she had been brought up to follow the drum? Until now she had prided herself on her ability to care for Papa's needs. His batman had looked to his personal belongings, of course, but as soon as she was old enough, Isolde had learned fast to do what she might to make him comfortable. In return, he'd taught her all the skills he would have taught a son. Until Madge came into their lives.

"Madge made me live like a female," she disclosed, with some reluctance, "but there wasn't anyone else. The colonel's wife didn't stay in camp and none of the other wives came to Holland. I heard they went to Ireland, but Papa wasn't sent there because we were still travelling back from the Cape. And Sergeant Quick died on board and that's when Madge and Papa —"

She broke off, horrified at what she'd been about to reveal. Dreading the inevitable question, she eyed Lord Alderton. There was nothing to be read in his face, although his gaze met hers. A faint frown formed between his brows and Isolde braced herself.

"You've come from Holland?"

Relieved to be spared embarrassment, Isolde seized the change of subject, falling over her words in an effort to divert him from the dangerous truth. "Papa died there. At Bergen. We lost, you know."

He nodded, the frown deepening. "Yes, I know. But that was in September."

"We were delayed. They let the women go, but we had to bury Papa and it took ages to organise because the colonel was guarded until our people managed to procure his release. I had to wait for the money. And then it took time to find a ship, and so…"

She trailed off again, unnerved by his steady regard. She wished there was a clue to his thoughts there, but he gave nothing away. Impelled, Isolde began speaking again, only half aware of what she said. "I never had a chance to be a lady, you see. When Mama died, Papa took me with him to France. We went to the Cape Colony from there and didn't come back for three years. I was growing up by then."

"You were fourteen, fifteen?"

"Fourteen. Madge made me wear petticoats."

Lord Alderton's poise broke and he looked startled for a moment. Regretting her hasty words, Isolde once again waited for a difficult question. It did not come. He gave a slight smile, and sighed in a way that sounded resigned.

"Then I suppose we'll have to start at the beginning. Let us hope my sister will consent to do the honours."

Apprehension crept back. "Is she like you?"

"Not in the least."

The dry tone was not lost on Isolde and her misgivings deepened. Before she could ask any more, his lordship stood up.

"What of your mother's family?" he asked, moving to the desk. "Where are they situated?"

A fresh wave of despair engulfed Isolde. He meant to send her away. She had not wanted to be here, but somehow the thought of going among different strangers, be they never so much her family, was even worse than the notion of staying here and learning how to be a lady.

She toyed with the temptation to refuse to tell him, or pretend she did not know. But he was turning his head towards her, looking across the room in mute question. She would have to say something.

"Cheshire. At least, I think that's where they are."

He frowned. "I thought you were Irish."

"Papa is Irish." She caught herself up. "Was. Was Irish."

He did not appear to notice her slip. "He met your mother in Cheshire?"

"I think so. The regiment was quartered there."

"What was your mother's family? Her maiden name?"

Isolde wanted to deny all knowledge of it, but those compelling eyes demanded an answer. "Mary Vansittart."

"What?"

Puzzled at the sharp tone, Isolde eyed him. "Vansittart."

The incredulous look was back, deepening Isolde's confusion.

"Do you tell me you are related to that family? Vansittart's brood? Who then is the fellow Vere to you?"

The fire in his eyes dismayed her. But curiosity prompted her to answer with truth. "Vere Vansittart? My mother's brother, I think."

Lord Alderton sank into the chair at his desk, his eyes never leaving her face.

"The devil he is! That bloodhound is trying to ruin me."

Chapter Seven

It took several moments for the realisation to sink in. Richard could scarcely believe that, in the very act of composing his difficult letter to the man, he had been disturbed by the advent of the fellow's niece. If his father had chosen to conspire against him, he could not have devised anything more diabolical. What an ironic twist of fate.

He became aware of Isolde's youthful features staring at him from across the desk where she was now standing. She looked white and pinched. And more than a little scared.

Richard struggled to suppress his unrest. The child was not to blame. She was an innocent victim in this coil.

He straightened, only now realising he had dropped his closed fists to the desk, leaning his weight into them.

"My mother should be ready to receive visitors by now. Shall we go up?"

The girl did not move. "What did you mean? Why is he trying to ruin you?"

Cursing his unruly tongue, Richard forced a smile to his lips. "Nothing at all. Or at least, nothing that need concern you. Did you not say you'd had no dealings with your mother's family?"

"Yes, but —"

"Then the matter need not trouble you. Come."

He came around the desk and made towards the door, but she seized his arm and he was obliged to halt.

"But don't you see? That means you can't foist me off onto them. And you meant to, didn't you?"

Richard found himself unable to withstand the plea in her voice. "I had made no decision. I was only looking at possibilities."

"And now that one is closed?"

He sighed. "We don't know that. My dealings with Vansittart need not have any bearing on your acceptance into the family."

She drew back, dismay in those eloquent eyes. Close to, Richard was caught by a better determination of their colour. Green-gold, with flecks of hazel. Or was it hazel with flecks of green and gold?

"Why do you stare at me?"

He pulled back from the unimportant question and sought for an excuse. "I was thinking … wondering…"

"Wondering if you'll ever be able to be rid of me," she supplied.

He winced. "Not that, no. But I do think it necessary to make contact with your family."

Isolde's lips turned mulish. "If what you say is true, you are already in contact with them."

"But not yet on your behalf."

The eyes challenged him and Richard gave an inward sigh. He turned for the door.

"Let me make you known to my mother and then we'll talk again."

She did not question him as he led the way through to the hall again and took the stairs to the first floor. Richard was glad of her silence, and a glance told him she was a little overpowered by her surroundings. Having lived here all his life, he was used to the rabbit warren of corridors and plethora of rooms, many of which remained unused for the better part of the year, if not altogether. He could imagine that to one unaccustomed to more than a camp billet or a tent, the house might be rather oppressive at first.

His mother's sitting room was situated at the corner of the building, where light poured in from two sides. Richard had caused it to be changed from a bedchamber when his mother became confined by her illness. A wheeled chair allowed her to be conveyed from her chamber along the corridor, and the chaise longue set before the fire provided warmth, rest and the refreshment of the gardens visible through the windows.

She greeted him with the warmth of her smile, and Richard thought she looked a little better than yesterday. He saluted her brow and stood back, allowing her to see Isolde, who had followed him closely, but remained standing by the near window, her flame hair a halo in the light.

"This is Miss Cavanagh, ma'am. Isolde Mary Cavanagh, to be exact."

His mother's gaze appraised the girl, and he guessed she was fitting the dimly remembered image of a child to the woman grown. His own thought surprised him. Seventeen was little more than a girl, although he was aware many a debutante of the same age might be found on the marriage mart.

"Miss Cavanagh, welcome. Or may I call you Isolde?"

His mother's warm tone drove the apprehensive look from the girl's face and the smile was like a sunbeam.

"Yes, if you please," she said, dropping a curtsy that he could not regard as anything but awkward. She was right. She did not have a lady's graces.

"Come and let me look at you."

Richard moved aside to allow the girl access, watching her face. Isolde's smile faded as she eyed his mother's thin frame.

"He said you were ill. What is the matter?"

Richard winced. Decidedly uncouth. No well-bred girl would be so impolite as to mention it. His mother did not take offence.

"It is the wasting disease."

Isolde's eyes grew round. "Are you dying?"

"Isolde!"

Her eyes flew to his, startled. He glanced at his mother and found her faintly smiling, though a tell-tale flush stained her pallid cheek.

"She is nothing if not forthright, Richard. Yes, my dear, I'm afraid I am indeed dying. No one likes to mention it."

Consternation flooded Isolde's features. "I beg your pardon. I don't know these things. Should I not have said it?"

Richard cut in. "No, you should not."

"It's not ladylike?"

"Decidedly not."

His mother held out a shaky hand. "Never mind it, my dear."

Isolde took the hand, but did not seem to know what to do with it. Richard hid a smile and pulled a chair up to the daybed.

"Sit with me awhile." She looked at Richard. "I've no doubt you have things to do. Send Pennyfather up for her when luncheon is served."

Relieved, Richard shifted back. "Don't tire yourself out, Mama."

"Isolde will fetch my maid to me if I become exhausted, never fear."

"Yes, I will."

Richard transferred his gaze to the girl. "Try not to agitate her."

She gave him a look he could not interpret. Then she nodded.

Relieved to have a respite to consider the ramifications of his discovery, Richard departed.

The moment the door closed behind Lord Alderton, Isolde dropped the dutiful pose. Clasping her hands tightly together, she faced the older lady with a determined air.

"He doesn't want me to be here. I don't want to be a burden. Please tell me what work I can do."

The frail lady before her looked taken aback, her brows rising in a way that made her look like her son. They had the same straight nose, the same eyes, though her cheeks were sunken in the thin oval-shaped face. Her hair was also dark, but lacked the lushness of his.

"You mean in this house?"

"No. I want to work, so that I can support myself."

The brows drew together. "Why should you wish to? Your father sent you here for protection."

"Yes, but that was to Sir Thomas de Baudresey, and he is dead." Realising what she had said, she drew in a shocked breath. "Oh, I shouldn't say that to you, should I? He was your husband."

"And your father's friend."

Isolde waved that aside. "It doesn't signify. This Lord Alderton was not his friend, and he doesn't wish to be saddled with me." She saw the frown deepening and took it for disapproval. "I suppose I ought not to ask you. I wouldn't, but there's no one else. And I don't know what it would be acceptable for me to do, being a lady. Not that I want to be one, but I see that I can't choose and there's no point in fighting it."

47

A wavering hand reached out and closed over one of hers. "My dear child, you cannot mean you wish to leave my son's protection? That would be foolish beyond permission."

"But I —"

She was cut off, the hand upon hers squeezing gently. "Pray hear me out, child. There are so few openings available to ladies in your circumstances. I cannot think you would care to become a governess or companion. And anything else is unthinkable. Besides, in either case you would be expected to know the rules governing female conduct, and I take it that is just the problem." She paused and Isolde felt the flush creep into her cheeks. "Or have I misunderstood you?"

Isolde shook her head with vehemence. "I don't know any of those things."

"Can you draw or sew? Can you play the pianoforte and sing?"

"I can sew," Isolde offered, glad to be able to admit to one useful skill. "I had to make and mend in the camp."

The hand holding hers relaxed a trifle, and a chuckle escaped Lady Alderton. "I have no doubt you were very useful to your father."

"Well, I was," Isolde insisted. "But it's no use expecting anyone to ask me to kill and skin a rabbit, because I know very well ladies don't do such things."

Lady Alderton was openly laughing and Isolde tried not to feel resentful.

"You are evidently an accomplished young lady, my dear, even if there is little requirement in England for such an ability."

Isolde sighed. "You mean I won't be able to find suitable employment."

Lady Alderton did not answer this. She kept her hand firmly on Isolde's and her voice became persuasive. "Do you know, Isolde, I believe you need only learn the rudiments of the art of being a lady. You are an original, and that is always refreshing. I dare say, if you were to go to Town for the season, you would become the rage."

Vansittart! The revelation still smouldered, along with the fire he'd been damping down. He'd been unable to make up his mind whether or not the fellow was a villain. It was hard to tell. The apparency of real need was superseded by the veiled threats Richard had recognised underneath the politely worded communications.

As the century's end crawled closer, Vansittart's demands grew more urgent. Like many others, he had bought into the sudden success of Ely Whitney's mechanical cotton gin in the Americas, snapping up shares in a plantation. With cotton being produced in quantity, demand was threatening to outstrip supply and Vansittart's American co-owner and partner, who ran the place, was hounding him for more capital.

Richard could only thank Providence that his father had not followed suit and bought into the venture himself. Instead, in his usual fashion, he had carelessly committed himself for a future investment should it be needed. As Vansittart claimed, it was now sorely needed: more land, more equipment, more workers. And that last was the point where Richard balked.

Even could he spare the promised amount to honour his father's pledge — which he could not without bankrupting his already endangered estates — he was suspicious of Vansittart's intentions. Would he direct the funds towards a darker purpose: the purchase of slaves?

The practice had fallen into disfavour, much to the triumph of the abolitionists, but it was increasingly clear that the rising success of the cotton industry had made slaves profitable again. The question was, did Vansittart care? Was his need of more workers a euphemism for more slaves?

Nothing would induce Richard to supply the man with blood money.

Opening the centre drawer in his desk, he extracted the letter he had not yet had an opportunity to complete. He read the words again, misliking the deprecating tone. He was convinced the man did not deserve as much.

Picking up the sheet, he ripped it across twice. Then he rose and crossed to the fireplace. One hand on the mantel, he watched as the pieces caught, flamed and swiftly blackened. Just as all desire to placate the fellow withered into ashes.

He held a weapon now. A bargaining chip? At the very least, the means to confront the man in person. He had Vansittart's wronged niece, and he would use her to the full.

Chapter Eight

Restless, Isolde prowled the corridors. She'd been at Bawdsey Grange for near a week, but it felt like a lifetime. The dawdling life suited her not at all and she was hard put to it to keep up the docile façade.

Alicia de Baudresey, whom Lord Alderton had appointed her chaperon, had not yet returned from London, and Isolde's days were spent at the side of Lady Alderton, whenever the lady was well enough to sit up and could be brought into her sitting-room. Isolde had tried to be of better use, but Lady Alderton would not permit anyone other than her maid or Mrs Pennyfather to attend to her personal needs.

Instead, Isolde was subjected to a series of lectures on the behaviour expected of a lady, more specifically a debutante. In her view, nothing could have been more restrictive. She listened, remembered when asked to repeat her lessons, and chafed inside.

She met with Lord Alderton only at meal times, where she put her newfound knowledge to the test. She spoke in demure tones, looked to his example for which utensil to use at any given moment, and followed his lead as he ate. She noted his irritation in the frown as she mimicked him, but held her tongue on the urge to comment upon it.

Rather to her surprise, she found herself looking forward to his lordship's company. He was unfailingly polite, if a trifle distant, but the lurking twinkle in his eye was endearing. Even if Isolde was uncomfortably aware that his amusement was at her expense.

"You are laughing at me," she accused once, on catching the ghost of a smile as she sipped at her wine in a fashion as alien as it was delicate, her little finger poised in the air.

The smile reappeared, wider this time. "Accept my apologies. I applaud your efforts."

"Am I doing it wrong?"

"Not in the least. It just seems so odd in you."

"But it's how your mother holds her glass."

"I am aware of that."

Isolde was inclined to be indignant. "Well, then?"

Lord Alderton sighed. "You need not copy her slavishly. It really does not matter how you hold your glass."

"I thought you were intent upon my learning to behave in a ladylike way."

His gaze did not waver from her face. "You are taking it too much to heart, Isolde. You need only learn how to go on in company, and —"

"But that is how to hold your glass and which utensil to use." Doubt smote her and she eyed him in bewilderment. "Isn't it? I mean, along with my curtsy and deportment and so on. What else is there?"

For a moment he did not answer, looking away as he took a sip of wine. Isolde watched his strong fingers curled around the stem, his lips touching to the glass and the dip at his throat as he swallowed. She felt breathless all at once.

Then his glance found hers again and time seemed held in suspension. She hardly heard what he said.

"It's a matter of social interaction, that is all. Saying and doing what is expected. No one will condemn you for a small error at the dinner table."

Isolde was unable to answer, her mind far from the need to become a lady. She had determined to pay heed to Lady

Alderton's guidance for one reason only. It would give her independence. The skills were needed if she was to support herself, and that had been her only plan, regardless of consequence.

A fine moment to discover in herself a completely different ambition, and an impossible one at that.

Relief came in the person of the butler, proffering a silver dish upon which reposed a selection of sweetmeats. Isolde picked one at random and laid it down on her empty plate. In the periphery of her vision, she saw Richard wave the dish away, and immediately chided herself for using his name in her head. Lord Alderton he was and must stay. Especially since she could not possibly remain under his protection.

He had said no word of her future, nor did she know if he had written to her family. She had not asked and he had volunteered nothing. Not that it mattered. Isolde resolved to be long gone before any plans he had could be put into execution.

This morning, however, she found herself at a loose end, and she began to wonder if it was going to be bearable to wait long enough to acquire the knowledge necessary to be able to support herself somehow. Lady Alderton was having one of her bad days and had sent a message by her maid. Isolde was under orders to sit quietly reading the prescribed book detailing the conduct to be expected of a young lady.

Rebelling at last, she laid the book down and started out of the little parlour assigned to her use — the same in which she and Madge had been taken upon their arrival.

Isolde had expected to miss her, but instead she found herself enjoying a surprising feeling of release. Madge had been kind enough, at least when matters went her way, but she'd neither attempted to take the place of Isolde's long-deceased mother, nor concealed her real reason for remaining at the camp after her husband died.

It had taken a few months for Isolde to realise what was going on, and she'd suffered torments of jealousy and rage before understanding at last that this was yet another of her father's needs, previously unfulfilled. It was one Isolde could not supply, and she learned to accept Madge's presence in their lives, if not with pleasure, at least with complaisance. But she could not forgive either of them for ousting her from her ruling place in Papa's affections, and the bitter loneliness had festered, leaving her bleak, but fierce in her determination to rely on none but herself.

As she paced, unknowing where she was going, her thoughts centred on the things she must know before she could leave. There was little chance she could learn enough to do what a lady might. Besides, who would recommend her for a companion or governess? The best she could hope for was a maid or perhaps a housekeeper. Nothing Becky did was beyond her abilities, though she could never manage a house this size like Mrs Pennyfather. She'd pumped Becky for information, without giving away her reasons.

"It's none so bad here, miss. Better nor a small place, for I'd be near on my own then."

"What do you mean, Becky? How small a place?"

"Any house as ain't grand, miss. Even a bachelor household needs a maid of all work. But she's to clean and scrub, shop and cook too then, miss. It's glad I am as I've a place here. It's hard, but there's plenty to share the load."

Isolde's mind was made up there and then. She could do all of those things, and she was used to hard labour. A maid of all work was the ideal solution. If necessary, she'd steal some of

Lord Alderton's monogrammed notepaper and write a reference for herself.

A shaft of light across the corridor caught her eye and Isolde stopped, glancing at the door, slightly ajar, from where it emanated. Creeping forward, she peeped into the room.

Panelled throughout, with shields, crossed swords and several antlered heads adorning the walls, and an open chequered floor, the room boasted little more than three or four straight chairs and a few cabinets. In one standing upright, Isolde saw a collection of long barrelled firearms.

The gun room? Her heartbeat quickened. This was more like! There did not appear to be anyone inside. She slid through the door with caution, her glance flicking about.

No, there was no one. Why then was the door open? An armoury was always kept locked. None knew that better than she. Which meant someone had been here, was possibly out for a brief space of time. Then she did not have long.

Heading straight for the gun rack, Isolde examined the weapons. Two muskets, a flintlock rifle and a blunderbuss. Moving to the glass-covered cabinet alongside, she peered in. Pistols! There were several, of different size and weight. Longing filled Isolde's heart and she fumbled for the catch to open the cabinet. It was locked.

Turning, she studied the crossed swords and shields. One would not use those for practice. Where were the foils? She caught a glimpse of steel in another open cabinet and hurried across the room. Yes! And they were protected, the tips buttoned.

With care, but eager, Isolde took one out and tested the weight, flexing the blade. Perfect. Grasping up her skirts in her left hand, she moved into the free open space and fell into the fencer's pose, making a pass.

How she'd missed this. All the frustration fell away, and Isolde's heart lightened with the familiar spring of her feet. Advance, lunge, retire. Ignoring the hampering skirts she was holding out of the way, she went through the drill, quartering an imaginary opponent as she dived and thrust, retired and lunged to thrust again.

Exhilaration rose inside. This was the life she craved. This was action, joy and living. This was —

Her guard faltered and she froze mid-lunge, the foil outstretched even as her eye shot to where she'd caught the anomaly at the edge of her eye. Lord Alderton was standing in the open doorway, regarding her with a face of thunderous conjecture.

Isolde's already leaping heart began to pound. She pulled her arm back, letting the point fall towards the ground as she wrenched her body into its normal posture.

His gaze dropped to her bared ankles, and Isolde let go her skirts in haste, smoothing them into place with one hand. For the life of her, she could not recover the air of docility she'd been wearing. Instead, she glared defiance, gripping the foil's hilt.

Recovering from his stupefaction, Richard noted the quivering lips in the white face, the brightness of the eyes that dared him to criticise.

He shut the door and strolled into the room, keeping his gaze upon her, his voice neutral. "Any other hidden skills I ought to know about?"

A sharp indrawn breath and a tiny frown. "You are not angry?"

He raised his brows. "Should I be?"

Her shoulders shifted. "It's not ladylike."

He allowed himself a faint smile. "No."

She said nothing, only surveying him with a lurking puzzlement he read with ease.

Richard did not move from where he stood. "Put the foil away. Or shall I take one myself and we'll see what you can do?"

Her chin lifted. "I'm not dressed for it."

His eyes travelled down the disarranged petticoats. Her words triggered a memory in his mind, but he let it go. He was sorely tempted to test her mettle. She was radiating defiance, but her eyes showed uncertainty. She had expected to be rebuked. On a sudden whim, Richard gave in to his baser self. "How would you dress for it?"

She eyed him, hesitant. He waited. Her head went up and her words rang. "In boy's clothes."

A laugh escaped him. "Indeed?"

"Of course. Skirts hamper movement, though I've fought in them before now. And one can't ride astride in a gown either. It's indecent."

That was it. Riding astride. She'd mentioned it before. His lip curled involuntarily.

"Yes, I should imagine it might well be."

The girl tossed her head. Had she misunderstood his amusement? Again? "I suppose you will say I must never wear breeches."

He took the wind out of her eye. "On the contrary. I was just going to suggest that you don them one of these days."

Astonishment mingled with suspicion in those expressive orbs. "Why, when you insist upon my learning how to be a lady?"

"I want to see how good you are with that weapon. It would give me an unfair advantage if I were to insist you engage in a bout hampered by your petticoats, don't you think? But not today."

She appeared to have difficulty taking in his words. Richard hid a smile and held out his hand for the foil. She relinquished it, hilt first, as a seasoned fencer should.

"Thank you."

He set it back in its place and crossed to the glass-covered cabinet. His desire to test her increased. Just how far from normality had this extraordinary life taken her?

He took the key from his pocket and inserted it into the lock, lifting the glass lid and setting the rod in place to hold it firm. "Come here," he commanded, without looking at her. In a moment, he felt her at his side and turned, waving a hand across his pistols. "Which would you choose?"

The girl's eyes met his, narrowing. "I prefer my own."

His lips twitched. "I should have guessed. Where do you keep it?"

"In my trunk." She grimaced, biting her lip. "At least, that's where I packed it. I always used to keep it under my pillow."

"Primed and loaded?"

"Of course. What is the use of an unloaded gun?"

He was hard put to it to keep his amusement in check. She had learned these lessons well, in any event, whatever she had not learned of feminine customs. He recalled what he'd witnessed when he entered the room. "Dare I suppose you have your own sword also?"

Regret entered her face. "I never had one of my own. I have Papa's sword, and his foils."

"Then I imagine they are now yours."

Her sunbeam smile threw him into disorder.

"I had not thought of that."

Richard was tempted to command her to give her weapons up into his keeping, but he was reasonably confident she would balk. Besides, he was loath to take more from the child than she had already lost.

The reminder of her youth gave him a jolt. Seventeen, and she had more knowledge of male pursuits than the feminine tricks she would need in her coming life. What was more, from items she'd let drop, and going by his housekeeper's judgement which should never be ignored, he was strongly of the opinion that Isolde had been fully aware of an amorous liaison between her father and Mrs Quick, who'd brought her here. It had not taken a deal of thought for him to work out why the woman had no desire to remain as chaperon, since the tie that had kept her had presumably been buried with Captain Cavanagh.

But no genteel debutante should have the smallest familiarity with such affairs. Little though she was to blame, she was totally unfitted for society. What in the world was he to do with her?

Reminding himself that it might not fall to his lot to decide, he closed the cabinet and locked it again. When he turned, he found Isolde had moved away, her eyes running over the arms decorating the walls.

"They are medieval, no longer in use."

She glanced back at him and then fixed her eyes on a shield above her on the wall. "Is that your coat of arms?"

Richard came to join her, letting his gaze wander over the quartered shield, with the bears, castle and gauntlet. "It's the de Beaudresey arms, but we no longer use them."

Her lips curved. "It's a finer name than Alderton. My father said it's very old."

"Norman. My ancestors were the invaders."

"Mine were fighters." Her eyes sparkled. "The Cavanaghs have always been soldiers." A sigh came. "I wish I'd been born a boy."

He had to laugh. "Yes, I can see that would have suited you a deal better. Don't repine, Isolde. You make a remarkable girl."

She turned startled eyes upon him and pink crept into her cheeks. He observed it with interest, not unmixed with amusement. It was plain she had no experience of compliments, nor, he guessed, did she expect any hint of admiration. It was both refreshing and sobering. She was like an unbroken filly, wild and vulnerable. Was his sister capable of handling her without destroying the gauche innocence that formed the chief of her charms?

Chapter Nine

"Have you taken leave of your senses, brother?"

The voice was shrill, rampant with fury. Isolde shrank into the lee of the staircase, unsure from which of the front rooms it was coming.

"My dear Alicia, you know full well it is not I whose wits have gone begging. You don't suppose I voluntarily assumed this guardianship, do you? This is our father's doing, not mine."

Lord Alderton's measured tones poured cold into Isolde's chest. Hadn't she known he didn't want her? After the interlude in the gun room yesterday, her desire to be gone from this house had felt a trifle eroded. She had been foolish to imagine Lord Alderton was beginning to like her. Remarkable, he'd said. She had hugged the word to herself, its effects warming the icy places. Only now did she see that it was not necessarily remarkable in a good way.

"Yet you insist upon dragging me into the business," came from the woman. "As if I did not have enough to worry about."

"It's only temporary, Alicia. Come, what would you have me do? The child is alone and friendless. I could scarcely turn her out."

"Child? She's seventeen, you said."

"But distressingly naïve. She had as well be fifteen for all she knows of how she should behave."

Isolde flushed where she hid in the shadows. She longed for the courage to make her presence known, or to run away so as not to hear more. But her feet refused to move from the spot.

"What, is she a savage?"

The woman's tone bore vicious scorn, and Isolde could only be glad of Lord Alderton's snapped response.

"Don't be ridiculous. She's been following the drum and no one has taught her the rudiments of ladylike conduct, that's all."

A high-pitched laugh pierced the air, false and filled with contempt.

"I thank you, brother. A fine task you have set me."

"I trust it will not prove beyond your capabilities." His tone was dry and Isolde recognised a timbre within it that told her there was little love lost between the two. "Mama has begun the work. You have only to add what her condition will not allow her to accomplish."

"Ha! You know nothing of the matter. If this creature is as ignorant as you claim, I will have my hands full. Not that I have as yet agreed to stir in the matter."

"If you won't help her in that respect, will you at least serve as chaperon while she is in this house?"

"I can scarcely do other, since my presence affords her as much. Whether I do more is yet to be decided."

Footsteps sounded, and Isolde slipped to the back of the staircase, close to the green baize servant door, her mouth dry, her limbs trembling. She heard the footsteps ascend the stairs and leaned against the back panel, closing her eyes against despair.

She'd heard the carriage while she was with the invalid. She wished she had not called Lady Alderton's attention to it. She would not then have been sent down to discover whether this betokened the return of the daughter of the house.

"Isolde!"

She jumped, eyes flying open as she turned in shock. She had not heard Lord Alderton's step. His frown was heavy and her breath caught.

"How much did you hear?"

Isolde swallowed her fright. "All of it."

"Damnation!" The breath sighed out of him. "She'll come around."

Isolde did not say she hoped the woman would not. The thought of exchanging Lady Alderton's offices for those of the unknown Alicia filled her with dismay and apprehension.

She cast about in her mind for relief and found the only possible option. "Have you written to my relatives?"

His features grew taut, and Isolde hesitated to mention the name that had evoked so much ire.

"Not about you, not yet."

She regarded him with growing dismay. "What will you tell them?"

"No need to trouble your head about it, child. Nor is there any rush."

"But you said Vansittart is trying to ruin you."

A smoulder grew in his eyes. "That matter need not concern you. It's a separate issue. However, now that Alicia is here and I will not be leaving you unprotected, I will be able to pursue that and other business awaiting my attention."

A hole opened up inside Isolde. She knew he didn't want her, and she was determined to go away, but the notion of him leaving her here unaccountably sank her spirits. "You are going away? Will you be gone long?"

"I hardly know. Unlikely, I think."

Isolde spoke without thinking. "I believe my relatives are in Cheshire. Should not you contact my grandparents?"

Lord Alderton's tight-lipped look softened a little and she saw compassion in his eyes.

"I am afraid they are both dead. I'm sorry, Isolde. Vere Greville, or Lord Vansittart I should say, is your nearest relative."

Shock hit. "Lord Vansittart? He is titled?"

"Your grandfather was an earl."

Her mind spun. "Then Mama was…"

"Lady Mary Greville. That is your family name."

She could not take it in. "But Papa … he never said… He said Vansittart. I thought it was her family name. He never told me it was a title, or that she was of such high birth."

"You don't remember her?"

"Yes, but she never spoke of her family. I didn't understand then that they had eloped." A chill ran through her. "That's why they cast her off. An earl's daughter. They will never acknowledge me. I can't go to them, Richard. I can't!"

She scarcely realised she had used his name. She only knew the last hope was gone. In the back of her mind it had been there, a last resort. But now, that disappeared with the rest.

She became aware that her hand was being held in a warm clasp. Richard's features were close, his dark eyes capturing her attention.

"You need not. Your father named mine guardian. He did not intend for you to go to them. I will honour his request, Isolde. You have a home here."

She could not speak. Her vision splintered and she heard the groan as he pulled her into the safety of his arms.

The embrace held for but a moment. Recalling his position vis-à-vis the girl, Richard withdrew, releasing her.

"I beg your pardon."

A tentative smile hovered, drawing his attention to her lips and an unwelcome stir within him. Her voice was husky. "For what?"

Richard winced. "If you don't know, that makes it worse."

Uncertainty crept into her eyes. "Should I mind it then? I thought you were just being kind."

"I was." He seized on the excuse. "Nevertheless, it was not conduct befitting a gentleman."

"Or a lady?"

"That too, but at least you did not know it."

Mischief flitted across her face. "My first lesson. I will remember."

The stir within intensified and Richard groaned in spirit. This damsel was a danger in more ways than one. The sooner he rid himself of the encumbrance, the better. Why in the world had he been so reckless as to assure her she had a home here?

He drew further away, intending to utter a dismissal. To his dismay, Isolde took a pace towards him.

"You won't go before our bout, will you?"

For a moment, he did not understand her. "Bout?"

"The foils? You wanted to try me, you said."

In the bustle of his sister's arrival, he had forgotten. He was about to reassure her, and was abruptly assailed by a vision of Alicia's face should she hear of it. And he had not yet persuaded her to take on the education of the girl.

"That must be postponed."

She surprised him. "Because your sister would not like it?"

He spoke without thought. "Shrewd of you, Isolde."

Those speaking eyes registered a hit, and something else. She looked as if she might say more, but was doubtful of its reception. Richard could not find it in him to ignore it.

"Don't look so dismayed. I won't allow you to be made unhappy."

She caught an audible little breath. "How can you stop it, if you are not here?"

How indeed? He resolved to have a word with his mother. If anyone could curb Alicia, it was she. While she could, she would shield the child, he knew.

He forced a smile. "You will have my mother's protection. You had best return to her room. I dare say Alicia will be there by now and you may become acquainted."

He turned towards his refuge in the library, but not before he caught the droop of disappointment in the girl's posture, the apprehension in her lively features. The temptation to loiter with her longer was almost irresistible, but it would not do. If he must figure as her guardian, for the present at least, he could not allow himself to be influenced by her vulnerability.

Behind him, he could hear her lagging steps as she made for the stairs, and he sighed with relief, not unmixed with regret. The last thing he needed was to succumb to the lure of a waif with neither breeding nor background to recommend her. An earl's granddaughter she might be, but without that acknowledgement, her social position would be uncomfortable indeed.

He could only be thankful his sister had come, despite her reluctance to assume charge of Isolde. He could follow up the brief note he'd sent to Vansittart, stating that he would do himself the honour of calling upon him in the near future. Fortunately, the fellow was not at his Cheshire estates at this present, but in a lesser establishment in Hertfordshire. He would leave tomorrow.

Chapter Ten

Subdued but with rising resentment, Isolde struggled to endure yet another scold from the lips of Alicia de Baudresey.

"I will not put up with your insolence, girl." A finger was wagged in her face. "And don't answer back. From now on, you will follow these rules, which should be simple enough even for you."

Isolde did not trust herself to answer. She would not look away from the woman's mean little eyes. She had been in Alicia's charge for two interminable days and already she was longing for Lord Alderton's return.

Relegated to schoolgirl status, she had been questioned and lectured to, obliged to furnish a catalogue of her upbringing and education, only to have it derided with snorts of displeasure and disgust. And today her preceptress had decreed she must begin upon practical exercises to improve her posture and learn to move like a lady. Isolde had been unwise enough to retort that Lady Alderton had already started to teach her as much. Retribution was swift.

"In future, you will speak only when spoken to. You will perform any task assigned to you without protest or complaint. You will do exactly as I tell you upon every occasion, and if I catch you slacking or lazing about, it will be the worse for you. Do you finally understand, girl?"

Isolde nodded.

"Well? Have you a tongue in your head? Did you hear me?"

"Yes." Isolde dropped her eyes at last, for fear her real feelings would show. "I understood you."

"Ma'am," added the woman pointedly.

What, was she a servant? She swallowed the insult. This was not the moment for defiance. "I understood you, ma'am."

"That is better." Alicia picked up a large book that she had brought into the parlour with her. "Balance this on your head and let me see your deportment."

Relieved that Lady Alderton had trained her in this exercise, Isolde took the book and found it easier to support it on the cap Alicia had decreed she must wear to secure her autumn locks. She walked carefully across the parlour and back again.

"You will practice until I return."

With which, Alicia swept from the room. Seething, Isolde took one more turn up and down the room and then caught the book off her head and threw it, with some violence, against the door.

"There! That's how much I care for your deportment!"

The door opened. Isolde gasped as Alicia entered to stand in the aperture, triumph in her blazing grey eyes.

"I knew it. You make a play at docility, but underneath you are a vicious little spitfire. Well, don't think you will get the better of me, girl. If I am forced to take you in hand, you will feel my wrath if you defy me."

Isolde put up her chin, though inside she trembled. Venom and spite emanated from the woman, and there was no one to take her part. Lord Alderton had gone, and his mother was too weak and ill to be troubled.

"You will not find me wanting — ma'am."

It choked her to add the appellation, but until she could make her own way, she must do what she might to appease the woman, who now smiled in a way that showed she was well aware of Isolde's state of mind.

"Very well, let it be so." She pointed to the fallen book. "Continue the exercise."

Under the creature's basilisk eye, Isolde retrieved the book, set it once again upon her head and resumed her careful walk.

This time, when the woman left, she maintained the pretence for a good few minutes, treading up and down the room as she kept the book balanced on her head, until her thoughts developed into revolving plans inside it.

What if she were to leave? Would it trouble Richard to find her gone? She caught herself up. No, she must persist in thinking of him as Lord Alderton. Else she might begin to depend upon his kindness, and she must not. No matter what he'd said about giving her a home, he had the intention of being rid of her, for had he not said he would contact her mother's brother, a man she'd thought of as Vere Vansittart until the revelation about the earldom? Was that where he had gone?

The question lingered. He had said nothing of his destination, only that he must be away for a space and that his sister would take care of her. Ha! Much he knew of that.

Or had he known? He must know his sister's temper? Perhaps he hoped Alicia would tame her into the kind of creature suited to this censorious world.

Her throat ached and she struggled to keep back the threatening tears. She did not belong here, or indeed anywhere. It was hard to feel unwelcome in every sphere. If she'd married one of the soldiers, she could have coped. But Papa would never have permitted her union with a common soldier and none of the other officers had shown the least disposition to like her in that way. Indeed, they treated her very much as if she were a young sister, if not a fellow officer, engaging her in swordplay for practise and challenging her to shooting matches. Sitting around a camp fire with a coterie of soldiers and officers together, quaffing wine and swapping stories of comic antics or derring-do, induced a feeling of camaraderie, rather than romance. She was treated with indulgence, but never a hint of anything untoward.

For the first time it occurred to Isolde to wonder whether that was due to her father's influence. Or to Madge perhaps? Once Madge had her in charge, and she was obliged to wear petticoats at least some of the time, she had rarely been permitted to partake of such companionable evenings. Only now did she realise she had been shielded from the possibility of male advances. Papa had not wanted her to marry into the military. Was that because he had secretly entertained the notion of her coming here to Bawdsey Grange to become a proper lady? Had this been his design all along?

Why had he not spoken of his ambitions for her? She could have told him how little she wished for such a life. She might have found a place for herself in the only milieu she understood. Now it was too late, and she had become a burden where she little wished to be.

A resolve formed in her mind and settled in her bosom. She would not conform. Let them understand that she was different. If Alicia de Baudresey supposed she could bully and mould her into something she was not, she would soon learn her mistake.

With which, Isolde allowed the book to slip from her head and set it down on the table. Opening the door with caution, she peeped into the hall. The coast was clear.

Isolde slipped out of the room and started towards the corridor. A flash of colour caught her eye and she looked up, freezing in place. Alicia was on the landing, in conference with the housekeeper.

The pit of Isolde's stomach vanished, despite her brave resolve. She eyed Alicia's back. She had not turned. With luck, she'd not heard anything.

But Mrs Pennyfather was facing her, she must be able to see her. Praying she would not look across at her, Isolde stepped backwards as silently as she could, keeping her eyes on the pair. She felt the door behind her and stealthily turned the handle just as the housekeeper's glance flicked once and caught her eye.

Isolde held her breath. An eternity passed. Then Mrs Pennyfather was once more regarding Alicia de Baudresey, who was still talking.

A soldier's daughter, Isolde knew when it was prudent to retreat. She whisked herself back into the parlour and let her breath go in a whoosh, leaning back against the closed door.

Defiance would have to wait.

Chapter Eleven

Vansittart's attitude was welcoming, but Richard remained wary. There was a calculating look in the fellow's eye that he mistrusted.

He was a man of some stature, although his waistcoat strained above a rounded belly and there was puffiness about the eyes, signs of middle age and perhaps a too fond addiction to the fleshpots. He wore the years well otherwise, and managed to appear at once urbane and conscious of his superiority.

Richard found himself disliking the man and strove for fairness. He had no knowledge of Vansittart beyond his letters, but the tone of these was evident in every motion and gesture.

"Make yourself at home, Alderton. I'll ring for refreshments."

His host moved as he spoke to the bell-pull hanging beside the fireplace and gave it a tug. Turning, he gestured to one of the spindly elegant armchairs set in the space before the fire.

Richard sat, watching the other take a seat, with studied grace, upon one opposite.

"You need not have taken the trouble to make the journey in such inclement weather, my dear Alderton. A letter would have sufficed."

Richard braced himself. "Not to discharge my errand."

The man's brows rose and he looked pained. "I am sorry to hear it. This does not augur well."

Not averse to a diversion from his true purpose, Richard chose to seize upon this opening. "I'm afraid it does not. To be blunt, Vansittart, to accede to your request — or should I say demand? — would ruin me."

A laugh escaped the other's lips. "You are very frank, sir."

"I have need to be. What is more, I cannot conceive why you should require my assistance, when it is plain you must have sufficient means of your own."

He described an arc with his hand, taking in the handsome proportions of the saloon in which he had been received. It was a large apartment, decorated with sparsity but elegance in the manner of Adam with his signature delicate white tracery against blue walls, a couple of slim-legged half-tables set against them and two neat sofas matching the chairs in which they sat, the cushioning picked out in brocaded blue.

"Ah, but appearances can be deceptive, my dear fellow. We contrive to present a suitable front, but an impoverished earldom is no sinecure."

It occurred to Richard that the décor of this room had not been evident in the hall, which, now he thought about it, had appeared rather dim and dingy in the winter light. A footman had granted him entrance to Greville House, making haste to usher him into this saloon before going to fetch his master. It was conceivable that the rest of the place would not bear comparison. And the Cheshire estates must cost a pretty penny to maintain.

Richard took instant advantage of the man's candour. "In that case, I confess I wonder at your participating in a scheme that demands a great deal of capital."

The tart note did not have any noticeable effect on Vansittart. He gave vent to a soft laugh.

"But in a bid to repair my fortunes, what else? And from what you say, if you are similarly circumstanced, I should suppose you would jump at the chance to secure a share."

Richard did not even try to keep the contempt from his voice. "In slavery? I think not, Vansittart."

For a split moment in time, the urbane expression vanished in a look of pure fury. And then the fellow was again smiling. "If that is what you understood, Alderton, I fear you are wide of the mark."

"Indeed? Then how would you explain the increased need for so-called workers?"

"Not merely workers, my dear fellow. We need machinery and land."

"And who will work that land? Who will sow and tend and pick your cotton on that land? You will need an increased labour force, will you not?"

"But you have quite misunderstood the matter, my friend. The investment is in the cotton trade, not in human trafficking. What sort of a fellow do you take me for?"

Richard chose not to answer this last, sticking to his guns.

"I am not utterly ignorant, Vansittart. The cotton plantations are manned by the forced labour of slaves. I can have nothing to do with such a project."

"Your father was not so nice in his views."

"Perhaps he did not fully comprehend the ramifications."

Vansittart's lip curled. "Oh, he knew."

He was silent for a moment, his features for once free of the false smile as he drummed the fingers of one hand upon his knee.

Richard took opportunity to study him and a slow sense of familiarity grew. Was there a hint of red in the shorn locks? Unlike many gentlemen of his generation, Vansittart had left off wearing a wig, preferring a natural style which utilised the curl of his pale brown hair in a fashion flattering to his undeniably good looks.

As if he became conscious of Richard's regard, the man looked up, triggering a flash of recognition. He had Isolde's eyes!

The abrupt recollection of his mission caused Richard to jerk into speech. "As I told you at the outset, sir, I did not come for this particular discussion. Or only in passing."

The man's brows drew together. "You dismiss it thus easily, Alderton? Your father made me a promise. Have you no honour?"

"Have you?" Richard returned.

Vansittart sat up with a jerk. "What the devil do you mean by that?"

"I will tell you."

Now the moment had come, Richard hesitated. He had thought of various ways to introduce the subject, but none of them came to mind. All he could think about was the image of Isolde's woebegone features.

He got up, unable to bear the comparison with this man — her uncle, if the business proved true. Did he doubt it? Isolde was ignorant of all but the family name, as she had supposed the title to be.

Crossing to a wide window, Richard looked out over spacious grounds. Had circumstances been otherwise, Isolde would have been well acquainted with them, with this house, even had she lived elsewhere. This was her rightful milieu, where she belonged. Yet he could not see her here. Not the unconventional girl she had become.

He became aware of the silence and turned his head. Vansittart had not moved, instead watching him with puzzlement in the eyes too like Isolde's for comfort.

Richard squared his shoulders. He must do this. She deserved no less.

He turned, facing the man and looking him in the eyes.

"I believe you had a sister once."

Shock sent the man's eyebrows soaring. "What in the world—?"

"Lady Mary Greville, I think."

Vansittart was on his feet. "I don't know what you mean by this, Alderton, but let me say here and now that I will brook no interference in my family affairs."

"Very proper, sir, but this matter happens to have fallen into my lap, and as it nearly concerns your family, I have no recourse but to bring it to you."

There was nothing of urbanity now in Vansittart's countenance, marred instead by a scowl. "Explain yourself, if you please. What do you know of Mary?"

"Nothing at all. Except that her daughter has been sent into my charge."

The man looked thunderstruck. "Her daughter!"

"Isolde Mary Cavanagh."

An ugly sneer creased the other man's mouth. "Do you tell me that snivelling rascal had the gall to try to palm off his brat upon me?"

"No, I tell you nothing of the kind," Richard retorted, furious at his reaction. "Captain Cavanagh sent her to my father. They were friends. It seems my father agreed to become her guardian should Cavanagh have the misfortune to lose his life."

"Dead, is he? I'm glad of that at all events. I'd have killed him myself had my father permitted me to follow them."

"I am not here to discuss the merits or otherwise of your family's actions in cutting off a daughter of the house —"

Vansittart was up, snarling in his response. "How dare you, sir, judge me? What do you know of the matter?"

"Have I not just said I know nothing? Nor am I judging you. I am solely concerned with the unenviable situation of your niece."

"My niece! She forfeited the right to that title when her mother eloped."

"She? She did so?" Contempt rode Richard. "Did she ask to be born? Was she present to object? Had she any say?"

The man had the grace to flush, but his features remained raw with anger. "Oh yes, Alderton, the sins of the mother redound upon the daughter. I can have no truck with Mary's brat."

"Then I can have no truck with your vile schemes."

A silence fell, and Richard heard the echo of his own words with dismay. He had forgotten his pettish resolve to use Isolde as a bargaining chip. When he came here, it was solely to see if he might restore her to her family for her own sake. But the words were out, and Vansittart was looking both stunned and thoughtful.

"Interesting." The urbanity was once again in place. "So much for your lofty words against slavery, Alderton."

"Nothing of the sort," returned Richard, irritated. "Nothing could exceed my dislike of the project."

A sneer crossed the other's face. "But if I will relent in the matter of my niece, you might reconsider."

"I did not say so."

"You implied it, my dear fellow."

Richard could not deny it. He waited, unwilling to concede as much. He had lost the advantage and it behoved him to delay saying anything until Vansittart showed his hand.

The man moved across to the table and picked up the decanter, glancing across. "Madeira?"

Feeling in need of the restorative, Richard nodded. Vansittart poured a measure of the wine and Richard moved to accept the glass held out to him. The other served himself and turned, the smile — in which Richard no longer held the slightest belief — once more upon his face.

"Let us sit. Perhaps we should begin again, my dear fellow."

Richard took his seat, and sipped at the wine, feeling a measure of calm return as the soothing warmth slipped down.

Vansittart took a gulp of his own drink and looked across. The smile did not reach his eyes. "What had you in mind for my niece?"

"To be blunt, I hoped you would welcome her into your household."

A pained look flitted across Vansittart's features. "Yes, well, I think I have sufficiently expressed my sentiments there."

"You have indeed."

A pause ensued. Richard would not give ground. Let the man make his own propositions. They were unlikely to find favour with him, whatever they might be. His dislike of the fellow was growing.

"Perhaps it would be politic for me to meet the girl."

"To what purpose?"

Vansittart lifted his chin in a gesture reminiscent of Isolde. "To find out what sort of creature she may be."

"Whether she is worthy of your notice, you mean?"

"My dear Alderton, there is no need to poker up. Can you not see how great a sacrifice I am making to my family pride?"

There could be only one response to this. "No, I cannot. I see only that you mean to use Isolde to further your own ends. She does not deserve that."

"Or even as much," snapped the other, his true colours seeping through.

Richard set down his half-empty glass and stood up. "I am wasting my time here."

Vansittart was on his feet. "Not so hasty, my friend. Our business is by no means settled."

"It is to me."

The other spoke softly. "Come, come, my dear Alderton, I am not a fool. You did not make this journey for purely altruistic reasons. Our business aside, you clearly have no wish to be burdened with some foolish promise of your father's to house an unknown girl."

It was true. Or at least, it had been. But having met Vansittart, Richard knew he could not abandon Isolde to the man's harsh and heartless attitude. He opted for the truth. "You are right, of course. But that burden is preferable to the one my conscience would suffer should I give her up into your care, Vansittart."

He might as well have slapped the man. Fury swept across his face, and Richard wondered for a moment if Vansittart would ignore the rules of honour governing such affairs and call him out.

It was an evident struggle, but etiquette won. One did not, as host, force a challenge upon a guest. The false smile was plastered back onto the man's face.

"We are not done, Alderton, so pray do not think it."

Richard curled his lip. "You would have me think the matter over? I'm afraid you will be disappointed."

"I am not a man who readily gives up."

"I had noticed. However, you do not know me, Vansittart. I am not like my father."

"That, my dear fellow, is patent."

Richard was obliged to laugh, and they parted in a spurious amity. Yet he could not shake off a faint streak of apprehension as he drove away.

Chapter Twelve

Isolde swaggered down the corridor, heading for the armaments room. She had not practised since Richard caught her in there when she first arrived at Bawdsey Grange. A few days had passed since her abortive declaration of war on Alicia de Baudresey. The woman's stern admonitions had not abated, and she had kept Isolde at it from morning to night. She'd had no notion how much nonsensical activity could be crammed into a single day.

If she was not practising her deportment or her curtsy and plying a stupid fan, she was fumbling through a catechism of rules and regulations she was forced to learn by heart only to be scolded for every mistake, every hesitation. Her fingers were numb and sore from struggling with her embroidery, her throat raw with singing. If one could call it singing, when one had to go over and over the same few notes only to be criticised for a tuneless ninny.

The life of a lady was evidently a dawdling affair, requiring useless so-called accomplishments which must surely bore any sensible man to death. Just as would happen to Isolde if she was forced to keep this up for much longer.

No Richard came back to save her, and she could not appeal to Lady Alderton, who was growing frailer by the hour. Isolde had had enough.

Defiance raised its head once more. In order to show Alicia who she really was under the spurious docility, it became desirable to practise her real accomplishments, correctly attired for the purpose. She had no opponent, but that need not deter her from drilling the familiar moves.

She had already resolved to inform Alicia, who would undoubtedly object mightily to her attire, that her brother not only approved, but had invited her specifically to wear them for an exploratory bout with the foils. Not that she would be believed, but it happened to be the exact truth, which she could prove on his return.

She met no one in her way, and was conscious of a riffle of disappointment. She'd hoped to confound Alicia while her courage lasted. But there was no sign of the woman and the house, as usual at this hour of the afternoon, was quiet.

A setback awaited her when she reached the armoury. The door was locked.

Was this Lord Alderton's doing? Or was it always locked when he was away? Frustration gnawed at her. She had not realised how much she missed the exercise. Her body longed for the freedom to lunge and thrust, to feel the lithe shift of muscle and sinew.

Balked, she aimed a kick at the unyielding door, cursing aloud. What should she do? It was too tame to retreat to her bedchamber and change back into the restrictive petticoats.

An idea surfaced. Why should she not use another room? She had Papa's sword and foils, did she not? She was on the move even as the thought completed, the image leaping into her mind, of the weapon securely wrapped and secreted at the bottom of her trunk.

She made short work of the corridors and had turned into the one leading to her bedchamber when a shriek of dismay stopped her in her tracks.

Turning, she beheld the maid Becky, hands at her mouth, her starting eyes fixed on Isolde's figure. The girl let out a gasp and her hands dropped. "Is it you, miss? Lord-a-mussy, whatever are you doing in them boy's clothes?"

Isolde put a finger to her lips, forgetting her resolve to confront Alicia de Baudresey thus clad. "Sssh! Don't give me away!"

Becky hurried up to her. "You'd best change quick, miss. If the mistress were to see you, she'd have a fit!"

Isolde lifted her chin. "I hope she does. Maybe she'll go off in an apoplexy."

Becky giggled, but she pushed Isolde in the direction of her bedchamber. "No chance of that, miss. Strong as a horse is the mistress."

Allowing herself to be shooed to safety, Isolde plonked down on the bed while the maid busied herself collecting up her discarded feminine garments.

"You'd best hurry, miss. The mistress sent me to find you and it's wild she'll be if you don't go to her straight."

Greeting this unwelcome piece of news with a toss of the head, Isolde began to unfasten her jacket. "She can wait."

Becky paused in her work and sent an anxious glance Isolde's way. "You don't want to make her mad, miss, I'm telling you. She wouldn't think nothing of taking a stick to you."

Ice slid down Isolde's veins. "She wouldn't dare."

"Oh yes, she would, miss. And she'd make me and Janey hold you while she did it."

A thumping started up in Isolde's chest as she watched Becky lay her female garments on the bed. She'd never been beaten. Papa had boxed her ears once or twice, but no more. But she'd seen boys being thrashed in the camp and heard their squeals. Would Alicia really use her so? Isolde did not care to put it to the test. She shrugged off her jacket.

"Why is she so horrible, Becky? Not that I expected anything less when I came here, but I thought it would be Lord Alderton who hated me."

Becky took the jacket and stowed it away in the trunk, saying it was best hidden where the mistress would not think to look. She was ready enough to gossip since it was plain Alicia was not much liked in the servants' hall.

"She don't like nobody, that one. Mrs Pennyfather says as she was ill-tempered from a child. Been worse, though, by all accounts, since that fellow cried off from the engagement."

Isolde unbuttoned her breeches and slipped them off, handing them to the maid.

"She was betrothed?"

"Years ago it were, miss. She had her chances, but as Mrs P says, she never took. Then her Pa fixed her up with some fellow, but he never made it to the church."

In the act of throwing off her shirt, Isolde stilled, shock hushing her voice. "She was jilted at the altar?"

Becky nodded, round-eyed. "Terrible it were, I heard tell. Them as were in service at the time said as how Miss Alicia's screams could be heard all over the county."

Despite the woman's cruel treatment, Isolde could not help a wash of sympathy. It was no pleasant thing to be rejected, as she knew to her cost. Perhaps there was some justification for Alicia's bitterness. Though it must have happened long ago, for the woman was not young. "How old was she?"

"On the shelf, miss," disclosed Becky, holding out the shift for Isolde to put on. "Past thirty."

"How is it she is so much older than his lordship?"

She threw her stays over her head and Becky seized the laces and began to pull them taut under Isolde's small breasts.

"They do say as there were babies in between, but her ladyship never carried well. She were lucky, Mrs P says, as she managed to produce an heir at all. But her ladyship were never strong after."

And now she was ill and dying. Which meant Alicia was the real mistress of the house. Did that compensate her for the lack of a husband and her own establishment? What would she do when Lord Alderton married?

Thought poised in her head as she contemplated the notion of Richard taking a wife. Why in the world should that make her heartbeat quicken? He was a peer with lands. He must marry in order to beget an heir. The wonder was he had not already done so.

Upon Becky urging her to hurry, she allowed the girl to help her on with the rest of her feminine attire. Cramming the hated cap on her head, she shoved her curls inside it and tied the ribbon under the chin.

"There, miss, you'll do now. Best come quick. The mistress is waiting in her ladyship's sitting room. I'll run ahead and tell her as you were taking a nap in your chamber."

Isolde thanked her and followed her from the room, dismayed to feel apprehension building again. The image of a beating, put into her mind by Becky, remained there, squatting in an uncomfortable corner. She could not but be glad that it was Becky and not Alicia, who had caught her wearing male clothing.

"My mother wishes to assess your progress," Alicia told her as Isolde entered Lady Alderton's sitting-room. The tone was neutral, but the grey eyes gave due warning of potential displeasure should Isolde fail to please.

"Yes, ma'am."

The submissive tone caused the woman to give her a sharp glance, but she made no comment, merely gesturing to Isolde to go to the daybed.

Lady Alderton's smile warmed her a little, but her ladyship's features were pale and Isolde thought she looked worse than when she had last seen her.

"I am sorry I have not been well enough to have visitors lately." It was said with an effort, the voice reedy and breathless. "But I understand you have made great strides, Isolde. Show me."

Feeling like one of the performing bears who had entertained the camp once or twice, she first sank into a curtsy and then, with a swish of her petticoats, sat down on the nearest chair with as much grace as she could muster.

"How do you do, ma'am?" she said, soft and polite as had been drummed into her by the task mistress who had her in charge. "I am sorry to hear that you have not been well. I trust you are better today?"

A little laugh rewarded her. "Bravo, my dear. You did that to the manner born."

Relieved, Isolde relaxed the stiff pose and gave an involuntary smile. "It still feels unnatural to me."

"That will pass. Alicia has taught you well."

Isolde said nothing. The lessons, conducted with nothing but criticism, had been a trial until her rebellion this afternoon. After Becky's revelations, Isolde could only be glad it had proved abortive.

She did not think her reaction had shown in her face, but she wondered when Lady Alderton looked across at her daughter.

"Leave us, if you please, Alicia. I wish to talk to the girl alone."

It was plain this plan was unwelcome. Alicia fidgeted, eyeing the elder lady with suspicion. At last she spoke. "For what purpose, Mama?"

An inflexible look entered Lady Alderton's features. "That is between Isolde and myself."

A dagger look came Isolde's way, which she interpreted as a warning: say nothing out of place, or else. It was plain, however, that Alicia had not gall or courage enough to gainsay her mother's expressed wish.

Isolde wondered at it as the woman went to the door, closing it behind her with a decided snap. Lady Alderton had not strength enough to compel her daughter in any way, yet it was evident she recognised her authority.

"She will not risk the possibility of my dying as a result of an altercation," said Lady Alderton, as if she'd read Isolde's mind.

It was out before she could stop it. "I should not have thought she cared." Recollecting herself, she at once begged pardon. "I should not have said it, I know."

But Lady Alderton was laughing. "You are nothing if not forthright, my dear, and as I'm sure I have told you before, I like that in you." She held out a thin hand and Isolde took it, slipping to her knees beside the daybed. The elder lady's eyes were kind, despite the weariness in them. "Don't let her bully you, child."

On impulse, Isolde spoke up. "Becky says she will beat me if I don't behave."

Lady Alderton's brows drew together. "Not while I'm alive."

"But you couldn't stop her."

"I don't need to. There are too many witnesses, child. Alicia would not run the risk of Richard finding out."

Then would Lord Alderton champion her against his own sister?

"Why should he care?"

Lady Alderton's loose clasp on her hand tightened. "Not know him yet, my dear? Richard is a man of compassion."

"You mean he feels sorry for me." Why the thought should make Isolde want to weep, she had no notion.

Lady Alderton's gaze became soft. "You don't want his pity. Will you accept his kindness?"

She would accept anything, could she but know it was done because he liked her a little, because he wanted her here. "I don't wish to be a burden."

Her ladyship smiled. "That old refrain, Isolde? I fear it is the lot of women to burden their menfolk."

The truth of this could not be denied, though it was no more palatable for all that. It struck Isolde then why Alicia would not risk alienating her brother. She was dependent upon his charity for her livelihood.

The fingers holding hers squeezed gently. "You dream of escape, do you not? Believe me, Isolde, your life would be a deal worse if you were to leave Richard's protection. Even Alicia would be preferable to that. Be patient, and let him take care of your future."

Sound advice, and Isolde wished she might persuade herself to abide by it.

"If it becomes too onerous," said Lady Alderton, "do nothing hasty. Come instead to me."

Isolde was grateful, and resolved to try to bear it until Richard returned. Surely he could not be much longer? She would not trouble Lady Alderton unless she had to, but it was comforting to have the option.

Next morning, that little comfort was snatched away. She was already awake when Becky brought her hot water, and she slipped out of bed only to be brought up short by the tearstains upon the maid's cheeks.

"Why, Becky, whatever is the matter?"

The maid caught her breath on the sob. "It's her ladyship, miss. She's gone."

Blankness invaded Isolde's mind. "Gone?"

Becky caught her breath. "She died in the night."

Chapter Thirteen

The butler's obvious distress when he opened the door alerted Richard. He wasted no time.

"What has happened?"

Topham's control slipped and he heaved a sigh. "It's her ladyship, my lord."

Richard's heart skipped a beat. He couldn't speak, only looked a question.

"I regret to have to give you such dismal news, my lord. She's gone."

Mechanically, Richard divested himself of his hat and greatcoat, handing them to the butler. The questions came without thought. "When did she die?"

"Last night, my lord."

"What time is it now?"

"A little after four, my lord. You are in time for dinner."

Dinner? An alien notion. He had no hunger, did not suppose he could eat if he was presented with food. "Has her ladyship's body been removed?"

"The undertaker has been sent for, my lord. Miss de Baudresey has taken all in hand."

"Has she indeed?"

"Letters have been despatched to your man of business and the doctor has been to certify the death."

But his sister had not yet effected a removal of their mother's body. Richard followed his instinct and headed for the stairs. When he reached his mother's room, he hesitated on the threshold, unwilling to face what he must find on the other side of the door. Thoughts crowded his mind.

He should not have gone. At least he would have been here in her final hours. Had Alicia treated her with kindness? Had she shown her due respect and care? Worst was the conviction his mother had died alone. Had he been here, he might have held her hand and eased her passage out of this world.

Too late. He had been absent at a crucial moment and he could never redress the fault.

He grasped the handle and pushed the door open, unprepared for the sight of the still figure lying in the middle of the four-poster. Riveted, Richard stared at his mother's form, shrunken in death. She was unnaturally straight, her arms close at her sides. He noted the curl of her fingers and his heart lurched. Someone had dressed her, shrouding her in a lavender gown he remembered from the days after she went into half-mourning for his father.

His thoughts spurred his feet and he found himself standing at the bedside, his gaze fixed upon the waxen face, its cheeks more drawn than he recalled, pale despite the application of rouge to her cheeks and carmine to her lips.

His gorge rose. Who had done that? A desecration. Mama rarely favoured such aids, especially in these months of her illness.

"I tried to make her look beautiful again."

The voice cut into his abstraction. He looked up. A face came into focus in the gloom on the other side of the bed.

"Isolde! What are you doing here?"

She did not speak, and Richard's harsh tone echoed in his own head. His eyes were adjusting, and he could see now that she was sitting on a straight chair at his mother's bedside, leaning forward, one hand cradling the still fingers.

What had she said? She had tried to make her beautiful again. He looked again at the travesty of red lips and cheeks and disgust roiled his stomach.

Instinct held him from bursting out against what she had done, the realisation at the back of his mind that her intentions had been admirable, if misplaced.

"I suppose you dressed her too?"

Isolde nodded, but her eyes bore witness to the impact of the tone over which he had no control at this moment. "I could not endure to see her in her nightgown. It — oh, it reduced her so."

She sounded apologetic, aware — afraid? — of his disapproval. Richard had an impulse to mitigate it, but he could not utter the words. His throat ached as the spurious unreality of the scene began to dissipate.

This was his mother, regardless of her garments, what she looked like. He had loved her, and she was dead.

"Go, if you please."

It was all he could manage. He wanted, needed to be alone.

His eyes were on his mother, but in the periphery of his vision, he saw the slight figure rise and slip out of sight. He waited until the door latch clicked, and then gave way to his emotions.

Dinner was a solemn affair, the silence punctuated only by the scrape of a knife on a plate, the clink of a glass, the stealthy footsteps as the servants moved about. And the occasional piece of information imparted by Alicia to her brother, who merely grunted in response.

Isolde, sitting mumchance in her place, and taking note of how little Richard partook of every dish, learned much to which she had not previously been privy.

Doctor Loader had expressed himself as astonished Lady Alderton had lasted as long. Mr Maxton — the lawyer? — had been sent an express.

"I desired him to hasten, and have hopes he may be here by the day after tomorrow."

Isolde was dismayed to learn that the undertaker had already sealed the coffin. She'd hoped to sneak back into the room to say her farewells, after having had to leave so abruptly.

"I desired him to wait in hopes that you would return in time, and you see I was justified. But there could be no further reason for delay once you had seen Mama for the last time."

On watch for every nuance in his expression, Isolde saw Richard's lips tighten. Was he angry at this haste? No, he must realise the body could not be left too long. Did he object to his sister taking charge? Or was it her conspicuous lack of sorrow that rankled?

Isolde looked in vain for any sign of mourning. Had Alicia even been back to her mother's room? Isolde had anticipated a tremendous scold upon Alicia finding out about her interference with her mother's corpse. Of all things, after she had done it, Isolde had dreaded that moment. She had not bargained for Richard's reaction.

A pang smote her at the thought. He had said nothing, but no words could have told her more than his expression and the way he asked the question. She felt his distress as acutely as if it were her own.

She could not regret her actions. How dreadful if poor Lady Alderton was sent to her grave in that graceless state of undress. Papa had been buried in full uniform, leaving the world as bravely as he had lived. Why Richard disliked it so much, Isolde could not fathom. She regretted adding to his distress, but she still believed she had done right.

When the repast was finished, Alicia stood up, looking across at Isolde.

"You need not wait up, child. Go to bed. I doubt we will foregather in the withdrawing room this evening."

It was couched in kindly terms for Richard's benefit, Isolde knew well, but the glint in Alicia's eyes assured her it was an order.

She rose and bobbed a curtsy, muttering a quick goodnight. She took care not to look at Richard while Alicia's attention was upon her, but left the room at once. She could hear Alicia talking. Then she need make no pretence of going to her bedchamber. Instead, Isolde crossed the hall on silent feet and slipped into her little parlour.

It was devoid of candles with no fire in the grate. The shutters were closed, the blinds drawn and the darkness was absolute. Isolde waited a moment for her eyes to adjust, and presently the outlines of the furniture became visible. She groped her way to a chair and sat down to wait, her ears attuned to hear the opening and closing of the door.

Alicia's footsteps very soon came out and she heard them ascending the stairs. All but the butler had left the dining room already, and he would remain until Richard had partaken of as much liquor as he wanted. Isolde had noticed that he drank freely of his wine, though he ate little. She hoped he would not succumb to his potations before she had a chance to talk to him.

The resolution of her future had become a matter of urgency. Without Lady Alderton, she was all too vulnerable to Alicia's spite. Not that she would tell him so. She hoped only to explain that without Lady Alderton, she believed it had become imperative to find her family.

Outside the library door, Isolde paused to dig up her courage. She knew Richard was in there, for she'd heard him dismiss the butler.

"Don't wait up, Topham. You may lock up now. I have some matters to attend to in the library before I retire."

Holding her breath, Isolde carefully turned the handle and gently pushed the door inwards, slipping into the room.

There was no one at the desk, but a pool of light from a single candelabrum centred on the armchairs near the fire, from where a faint glow still emanated. She could see a pair of booted feet crossed at the ankles, but Richard's face was hidden by the wing of the chair.

Isolde closed the door with care, and crossed silently towards the fireplace. She reached the chair opposite and checked there, looking across at him.

His eyes were open, but he did not appear to have noticed her. His chin was sunk a little on his chest and he seemed to be lost in thought, his hands loosely clasped together in his lap.

She was tempted to leave as silently as she had come, but the dejection in his pose stayed her. An urge to comfort him swept through her, but of course she could not go to him and draw his head against her bosom.

Recalling her father's sad demeanour in the days after her mother died, she thought of the next best thing. Looking about, she located a tray on a sideboard to one side. It contained several decanters.

Isolde crept stealthily to the sideboard and studied the silver labels set upon the decanters. It took a moment to locate the brandy. She picked the correct glass and poured a measure.

Turning, she found Richard's eyes on her. A jolt shot through her, but she quashed the flurry of nerves and smiled at him. No longer troubling to keep her feet silent, she moved to the chair and stood before him, holding out the glass.

"Here. Drink this. It will revive you."

He took it, though his brows drew together. He seemed about to speak, and then perhaps thought better of it and instead took a sip of the brandy.

Isolde turned and took a seat in the armchair facing him. She found him watching her. She spoke, the hush in her voice instinctive. "I know how you are feeling."

"You can't know."

It was rough, edged with grief. Isolde's heart ached for him, but she said nothing more.

For a moment his frown held. Then he gave a long sigh and his body relaxed.

"Forgive me. I forgot you are also recently bereaved. Of course you know."

She waited, giving him time, remembering how hard it was to speak of her despair. But when he said nothing, she could no longer remain silent.

"It will ease, Richard. For a time. You won't have leisure to feel it for a while."

He nodded, as if the effort to respond demanded too much of him. He sipped again at the brandy and it seemed to fortify him. His eyes found Isolde's.

"Why aren't you in bed?"

She felt the flush rise in her cheeks and was glad of the poor light provided by the candelabrum. "I wanted to talk to you."

"About my mother? I'm not ready to discuss it."

The dismissal was like a pin prick in her breast, but Isolde ignored it. "Not about your mother. I wanted to ask if you'd had word from Lord Vansittart."

His stare became intense. "Now? At a time like this?"

"What better time?" Isolde was aware her voice had sharpened, but she pressed on. "It's a distraction, isn't it?"

"Not one I need."

He looked away. Evading her? Why? She would not be deterred.

"Did you write to him?"

Richard's frown grew deeper. He kept his eyes on the liquor in his glass. "When the time is right, I'll pursue it. Not now."

Isolde's frustration surfaced. "But you must, Richard. I can't stay here. Without Lady Alderton —"

She broke off as his gaze turned back to her, his eyes hard.

"So that's it. And I was fool enough to think you were here to offer sympathy."

"I am," said Isolde, dismayed. "I do offer it. But —"

In one fluid movement, he stood up, setting the glass down on the mantelpiece with a snap. "You may rest assured that my mother's death in no way changes my responsibilities towards you. I have said I will take care of your future. Believe that I meant it."

Isolde stared up at him, her pulse wild in her veins. What could she say? He had misinterpreted her actions. It was unjust, but he was grieving. She made one last effort. "You don't understand…"

"Go to bed, Isolde. We'll talk of this another time." With which, he turned away, leaning one arm along the mantel and gazing into the fire.

Feeling alienated, and not a little guilty, Isolde pushed herself out of the chair. He did not look at her.

"Good night, Richard," she said softly, and left him.

Chapter Fourteen

The bustle was evident all through breakfast. Isolde would have known something was afoot, even if Richard had not announced his imminent departure.

"I must go to London."

Cold seeped into Isolde's veins. Despite his altered manner towards her, she could not stop the question, and knew her dismay was in her voice. "London?"

He did not look at her. "There is a great deal to do, and Maxton cannot proceed without me there."

Isolde cleared an obstruction from her throat. "How — how long will you be gone?"

His gaze flickered towards her and away again. "A few days, I expect."

Don't go, Richard. Don't leave me here with her.

She had to clamp her lips closed to prevent the words from escaping. Her gaze roved his drawn features, the lush dark hair that looped onto his cheek, the severity of his black cravat. He turned his head and his eyes met hers, and held. She could not read them, but she saw them change, soften. He opened his mouth to speak.

"Your man has finished packing, Richard, so you need not delay."

The contact broke. Richard looked across at Alicia as she entered the room and Isolde drew in a tight little breath and looked quickly down at her plate. In the periphery of her vision, she saw the black-clad form take her seat on the opposite side of the table.

"I've ordered the coach to be at the door within a half hour."

Isolde reached for her coffee cup, and saw Richard's frown appear.

"I was planning to drive myself."

"In this weather? Bad enough to be making the journey at all, though I know it can't be helped. Your groom swears it will come on to snow before the day is out. You would freeze in your curricle."

The coffee helped Isolde recover a little of her composure, and she took a surreptitious look from Alicia's triumphant features to Richard's stony face. Did he resent this ordering of his journey? That he didn't speak suggested he did not feel it worth his while to argue.

Isolde had noticed several such instances of the brother and sister rubbing against each other in the days following their mother's passing. Both had donned mourning almost immediately, and without being told, Isolde resumed the blacks she'd worn for Papa. She'd put them off once she left Holland and was no longer obliged to make a show for form's sake. Papa could not abide the custom and Isolde had scant regard for society's rules. But she was no longer mistress of her own actions, and she knew she would be expected to wear black at Bawdsey Grange.

Neither Alicia nor Richard had time for her, and Isolde had kept out of the way, employing the empty days with the stitchery imposed upon her before Lady Alderton died. She had once sought to find a book to read, and went into the library when she thought Richard was absent from it, only to find him seated at the desk, writing, a pile of papers to hand.

Isolde made to retreat, but he looked up and caught her.

"What is it?"

The curt note was disturbing, although she was growing used to hearing it from him ever since the night after Lady Alderton died. No opportunity had arisen for her to have further speech with him. Indeed, she scarcely saw him, except at meals. She might have been a ghost, for all the attention paid to her in this house.

"I just wanted a book," she got out.

"What sort of book?"

She was tempted to say any book, but she did not want him to know how much his attitude oppressed her. "Just — something diverting."

The frown did not leave his brow and his stare bored into Isolde. Then he threw out a hand, still holding the quill, and pointed towards the other side of the room. "There are some novels in that bookcase. At the end, on the middle shelf, I think."

Then he bent his head and resumed writing.

Isolde hesitated, her gaze following the motions of his pen across the paper. Should she apologise? Would he relent towards her? She cleared her throat. "Richard…"

He did not look up. "What is it?"

"I didn't — it wasn't — I never meant…"

Her voice died. She could not get the words out.

Richard's pen paused and his eyes rose to meet hers. Was there a flicker of a smile?

"I know. It doesn't matter."

Then his attention returned to his task and Isolde's heart sank. It was not the response for which she had longed, in the lonely night hours when she imagined what she would say to him. But at least he had forgiven her.

She waited a moment, but he took no further notice of her. She crossed quickly to the bookcase he had indicated, hunting through the titles on the shelves without really seeing them, her heart thumping, her eyes pricking.

Acutely aware of him at the desk, she made a pretence of searching while covertly watching him from under her lashes. He neither lifted his head, nor ceased his labours with the quill.

Tears squeezed out from under Isolde's lashes and she swallowed on a rising sob. She could not weep in his presence. Seizing a volume at random, she sprinted for the door, making it through and shutting it behind her before the tears spilled over.

She'd hurried to the small front parlour which had become her headquarters, and spent half an hour struggling to suppress the bout of misery that attacked her.

Thinking of it now, and of that shared instant a moment ago, she could not help a rise of hope. Was he melting a little towards her?

She stole a glance at him and caught him watching her. He turned his eyes away instantly, but not before she had seen the question in them. Her spirits rose a little. Only to drop again a moment later.

"Isolde."

She looked up. "Yes?"

"I desire you will resume your studies with Alicia while I'm away."

Isolde could not keep her glance from flying to Alicia's face. The woman regarded her with disdain in her eyes, though her mouth smiled. Isolde began to feel oppressed all over again.

"You cannot avoid the necessity to behave correctly," Richard went on, "whatever we decide about your future."

"We?"

It was out before Isolde could stop it. He ignored the question as if it was of no importance. Who were we? If Alicia was included, Lord help her!

He turned to his sister and she held her breath.

"I appreciate, Alicia, that with the funeral and all you've had to undertake, Isolde's education has been necessarily neglected, but it cannot now be delayed."

Her education? Was that how he saw it? Isolde had to bite her tongue not to burst out. Did he suppose her wholly ignorant? Not only could she read and write, Papa had taught her the rudiments of Latin and Greek too, not to mention mathematics, science and the tactics of war. Soldiering was largely a dull affair, with long days of inaction interspersed with marches and the odd battle. She'd had no governess and Papa had been her tutor, sharing all he knew just as if she'd been his son. Hours had been whiled away in this fashion.

"Have no fear, brother. I'll take care of it."

Alicia's voice recalled her. The woman's look spelt venom to Isolde and she flinched. There was a silence, and then Richard spoke again, a wealth of meaning in his tone.

"I hope, my dear sister, you mean you will take care of Isolde. I am leaving her in your charge, and I expect you to deal with her as I would myself."

Which was not saying much, if Isolde was to judge by the way he had treated her lately. She had brought it on herself, but that made it no easier to bear. Did he still believe her to be selfish and thoughtless? She wished he had at least given her a chance to redeem herself. If only he was not leaving so soon, for he did seem to have softened a little towards her.

"Brother, you may rely upon me."

The unctuous tone sent shivers through Isolde, and dread of the coming days began to overtake her.

All was set and Richard gave his final instructions to his butler, who told him the groom and coachman would have the travelling carriage at the door in a trice.

"Excellent. I may trust Reeve to see all is as it should be."

"Indeed, my lord."

Topham put a hand to his mouth and gave a discreet cough. Richard looked a question.

"Mrs Pennyfather has caused a hot brick to be placed in the coach, my lord, along with the travel rugs."

"Good God! Does she suppose I am made of sugar?"

The butler permitted himself a small smile at this sally. "You will appreciate, my lord, that all your people are determined to carry on as if the mistress was still with us. She would have ordered as much."

A pang smote Richard, but he suppressed it. His mother had ever been inclined to mollycoddle her only son. He had chafed at it, but now he realised he was going to miss her motherly concern.

"True enough. Thank Mrs Pennyfather for me, will you?"

The butler bowed and opened the library door. "If you are ready, my lord?"

There was no further need for delay, but Richard was conscious of reluctance to leave the house. A nagging image of a white face with a tell-tale trail of wet across its cheeks crept out of the corner where he had tried to banish it. He'd been harsh, and knew it for a kind of defence to enable him to keep his distance. But now that he must leave the child in Alicia's hands for a space, his conscience pricked him. She'd had an unhappy time of it, and his sister was unsympathetic.

He paused in the hall where Fareham was waiting with his outdoor clothing. He allowed the valet to help him into the great-coat, but on impulse held up a hand when he was offered the hat.

"One moment."

Crossing to the door to the little parlour, which he knew had been given over to Isolde's use, he gave a gentle knock. There was no reply. Richard grasped the handle and opened the door. A glance about the room immediately revealed its occupant perched in the window seat, staring into the grey mist outside.

She must have heard him, for she turned her head and looked across at him with eyes drowned in misery.

His heart contracted. Without thought, he closed the door behind him and crossed the room in a few swift strides. He saw the startled look leap into her face as he caught her up, and then it was buried in the folds of his great-coat as he clasped her close against him, murmuring words that came out with no purpose other than to comfort.

"Hush now, hush, don't weep! All will be well, I promise you."

He heard a doleful sniff and released her, digging for a handkerchief. Finding one, he held it out.

"Here. Dry your eyes, Isolde."

She took it, her breath shuddering a little, and brushed hastily at her wet cheeks. Her voice was husky when at last she managed to speak. "Thank you… I'm sorry to be such a ninny."

He smiled. "We are all of us allowed a moment of weakness."

Her candid orbs met his, contrition in them. "I hurt you. I didn't mean to."

"No, you didn't hurt me. I was grieving and I couldn't think straight. Forgive me."

Her sunbeam smile appeared. "If you forgive me."

Richard was hard put to it to refrain from pulling her back into his embrace. He rested back on his heels to put a little space between them. "Now we have that settled, will you promise me not to give way to melancholy while I'm away?"

A grimace crossed her face. "I'll try."

"And don't trouble your head about your future. I will take care of you." He had no difficulty in reading the doubt in her vivid eyes, and added on a teasing note, "After all, I am your appointed guardian."

He was rewarded with a tiny laugh, but the doubt remained.

"But you don't wish to be, do you?"

"We'll discuss that on my return. I haven't forgotten about your family either. We'll address all these matters in due course, if you will only be patient for a little while."

Her gaze did not waver, and it struck him that she was much more confident than her air of fragile innocence suggested. Her thoughts were not mirrored in her face this time, however, and Richard was puzzled.

"What is it? What are you thinking?"

A flush crept into her cheeks and she looked away. "I can't tell you that." Then her eyes returned to his. "I might one day."

He could not forbear a smile. "You intrigue me."

She put out a hand and he took it and, without intent, lifted it to his lips.

"Be good, Isolde."

Releasing her, he turned for the door.

"Richard."

Halting, he looked back. "Yes?"

She was frowning. "I may not be a lady, but I am educated, you know. More than most girls, Papa said, for he taught me as if —"

"As if you were a boy? Yes, I rather gathered as much."

"You said I had to continue my education."

Sighing, Richard turned. "Have I offended you?"

"Yes."

The defiant little word was oddly touching. He hid a smile and made her a small bow. "Then once again I beg your forgiveness."

She inclined her head and he had to laugh.

"Isolde, you are an original, I'll give you that." He moved back to her and held out his hands. To his mingled surprise and satisfaction, she put hers into them. "Will you, to please me, try to learn of Alicia? I know she is a little … difficult. But she does know what will serve you in society."

Her lips quivered on a smile. "Will it please you if I become a lady?"

He hardly knew what to make of that. Did she really care? He let go of her hands. "It's for your sake as well as mine."

She regarded him, rather enigmatically, he thought. Then she dropped a perfectly placed curtsy. "Have a safe journey, my lord."

He laughed out, and turned once more for the door, feeling a little reassured. He grasped the door handle and pulled, only then realising that the door had been slightly open. Had he left it so? He could have sworn he closed it and Isolde had called him before he reached it.

Faintly puzzled, he left the room, making sure of the clicking latch before releasing the handle. His valet stepped forward with his hat and gloves, and Topham moved to the front door. As he took these articles from Fareham, he discovered his sister standing in the aperture to the dining-room across the hall.

An odd expression flitted across her face as she met his gaze, and the suspicion struck Richard that she had been at the parlour door. Had she eavesdropped on his conversation with Isolde?

Then she was moving to him, smiling and wishing him a successful venture.

"Take no risks, Richard. It cannot matter if you are delayed. I will ensure we are fully prepared for Christmas. It will naturally be a quiet time, but the usual observances must still be met."

He agreed to it, took her proffered hand and wondered if he should again solicit her kindness for Isolde. If she had been listening… He tried to run his mind over what had been said, and could not recall anything beyond the last sight of Isolde's smile.

"The coach waits, my lord. You will not wish to keep the horses standing."

The butler's faintly admonishing tone recalled him and the moment was lost. A hasty goodbye and he headed for the front door, drawing on his gloves against the sudden biting cold.

Chapter Fifteen

Three interminable days and Isolde was ready to scream. Abandoning the chapter on precedence in the book of etiquette she was supposed to be studying, she paced the little parlour, trying to warm up as much as anything else. The fire was inadequate to cope with the cold pervading the house since the bout of heavy snow that had fallen late on the day Richard left.

Isolde had squandered fruitless hours worrying over whether he had managed to get to London. Topham, when questioned, had said it was not more than a day's journey, unless the weather was inclement. It could not be less so, in Isolde's opinion. What if Richard had to take refuge and was snowed in? He might not be in London yet. Lord knew when he would be able to return.

Suppose he did not get back for Christmas even? Not that Isolde anticipated any enjoyment from the festive season, with the alien environment in which she was incarcerated shrouded in mourning. Her hopes had not been raised by discussion with her usual source of information.

"I dunno, Miss Izzy, what with her ladyship gone and the mistress lording it over the place like she is," said Becky, who had abandoned all pretence of the servant to lady relationship with Isolde, much to her joy since the maid was her only friend in Bawdsey Grange.

"But what did you used to do?"

"Well, it ain't been no picnic these last two years, what with the master gone and her ladyship laid on her sickbed like, but Mrs P made sure as we had our goose and plum pudding dinner in the hall as ever was, and the mistress — Miss Alicia as we called her then — made sure as we got our Christmas boxes all right. Leastways, like Mrs P says, it were her ladyship what ordered it and Miss Alicia done her bidding, so it's as like to ninepence as we won't get nothing this year."

Isolde balked. "No, no, Becky, I am sure you will. Richard — I mean, Lord Alderton — would never permit such a thing to be forgotten. Indeed, I should not be surprised if it was not he, rather than Alicia, who arranged for it."

"I hopes as you're right, Miss Izzy, only his lordship ain't here, and Mr Topham warned as he might not get back in time."

A hideous thought that was already haunting Isolde's restless nights. The notion of spending Christmas with only Alicia for company made her resolve to hide in her room for the duration.

"But what of the gentry, Becky? How did they spend Christmas?"

Becky brightened. "With her ladyship in her sitting-room mostly. Mrs P had us make it cheerful like, with holly boughs and fir cones and such around the fireplace. Her ladyship liked to play at cards or fox and geese, and then she'd be wheeled to the dinner table for as there'd be gentry invited from round about, and before she took so ill there'd be one or two to stay. Cousins, I think. When his late lordship were alive, it were a regular house party and everyone merry as grigs."

But there would be no house party this time, and no dinner guests either. Isolde knew the neighbouring gentry had already paid their respects, and the funeral had been well attended. No family members had materialised, as far as she knew, but like Alicia, she'd not been there. Another lesson. Ladies were neither expected nor required to attend the funeral or follow the coffin. Isolde could not imagine how she would have felt if she'd been barred from seeing Papa off on his final journey.

Worse than any of this, however, were the incessant scolds, the sheer rudeness of Alicia de Baudresey. Relentless in pursuit of Richard's aim to educate Isolde into a lady, Alicia chivvied her ceaselessly, criticised every effort she made and never uttered one word of praise, regardless of how hard Isolde tried. Had it not been for the thought of Richard's inevitable disappointment in her, Isolde would have given up altogether.

She paced, rubbing her arms, and recalling Alicia's response the one time she'd lost patience and dared a protest.

"Why are you so cruel to me? What have I ever done to you?"

Alicia's mouth became pinched, her eyes narrowing into pin-pricks of malevolence.

"You are a dangerous upstart. Don't think I don't know what you're up to. I've seen the way you look at him."

Shock roiled through Isolde, accompanied by a wave of guilt. She'd never framed the thoughts, never for an instant looked at a possibility — a hope? — that lay coiled in unguarded ignorance somewhere deep inside. But at these words, it sprang full-blown into her head and she could not deny its portent.

Her face must have given her away, for Alicia's lips curved into a smile as unpleasant as it was knowing.

"Ah, you see, I was right." She snorted. "You are baying for the moon, girl. You will never be mistress here. You will never oust me."

Isolde found her voice, recovering the native rebel within. She lifted her chin. "I don't know what you're talking about."

"Oh, you do. I saw it from the first. Even my mother, God rest her soul —" said with a scornful inflexion that made

Isolde wince — "had started weaving plans in her head. I soon put a stop to that."

How? What had she done? What had been said? Or was it only Alicia's vengeful mind that thought up these things? It was all nonsense, of course. It must be. Impossible to believe that Lady Alderton had any idea of...

Isolde's mind balked. She would not even think it. Alicia had taken leave of her senses, so twisted that she saw shadows where there were none.

"If that is what you think," she managed, speaking with care lest her burgeoning emotions get the better of her, "I am surprised you are making an effort on my behalf."

Alicia let out a harsh laugh. "On your behalf? Don't be ridiculous."

Then it hit. "How could I be so stupid? You are doing it because Richard expects it of you. Because if you don't, you are afraid he will cease to support you." She saw by the fury in the woman's eyes that she had hit the mark. "You wrong him. He's not like you. However he felt, he would never cast you aside."

"No, he won't," said the woman, recovering herself, "because the opportunity will not be granted him."

With which, Alicia had turned and stalked from the room, slamming the door behind her. She had returned an hour later and carried on as before, just as if the episode had never happened. This morning she had set the passage for learning and left, saying she had other duties demanding her attention.

The night had found Isolde tossing, her thoughts in chaos, Alicia's words going round and round in her brain. She could not rid herself of the stupid notion the woman had about Lady Alderton. It was ridiculous to suppose there could be any truth in it. Yet Isolde kept remembering how Lady Alderton, that last night, had urged her to put her trust in Richard, to depend on him, on his kindness.

She clung to the memory of what had passed between them just before he left, and the knowledge that he had purposely sought her out. He had promised he would take care of her, and asked her to be patient. Take care of her how? As her guardian? Or only until he had persuaded her family to take her off his hands?

No, that was unfair. Had he not said early on that she had a home here? But nothing had ever been said to lead her to think there might be more between them, despite the disturbing products of her imagination. What could Richard possibly see in her, a creature wholly unsuited to life in his milieu?

The unacknowledged dream receded. If Alicia supposed her brother to have any amorous intention towards her, she must have windmills in her head. He was far more likely to palm her off on this Uncle Vere, Lord Vansittart.

Isolde sighed. If Richard did not want her, even that would be better than a future spent within these walls, subject to growing unhappiness and prey to Alicia's taunts.

She became aware of the near numbness of her limbs. She could not continue thus. She was clad in an old woollen gown of blue kerseymere, having left off her blacks today as they provided less warmth. But she needed a shawl.

Alicia was busy elsewhere. Isolde had no hesitation in leaving the parlour. She headed for her bedchamber.

She could hear the sounds before she opened the door. Isolde could not put a name to them, except that they betokened the presence of someone inside her room. Thinking it must be the maid, she turned the handle and pushed open the door.

A scene of chaos met her startled gaze.

Her trunk was open and someone was bending over it. A collection of clothes was thrown higgledy-piggledy across the bed. Several books had been hurled pell-mell to the floor and lay open, upside-down, their pages squashed.

"What in the world —?"

The woman straightened and spun round. Isolde stared at Alicia de Baudresey, bewilderment giving way to wrath as the creature's eyes met hers. She flung out an accusing finger towards the pile on the bed.

"Do you dare to tell me those are yours?"

Ignoring the question, Isolde started forward. "What are you doing? How dare you rummage in my trunk? What gives you the right to touch my things?"

Reaching the woman, she was met by a vicious blow across the face that made her stagger. Isolde grabbed hold of the bed post, wincing against the stinging pain. She was given no chance to regroup. Alicia came after her and delivered another swipe that felled her.

Isolde landed backwards on the carpet, her hands going out to break her fall. One banged onto the spine of a fallen book and a sharp stab accompanied the smart across her arms and breast where Alicia's second hit had caught her. Dazed, she stared up at the woman as she loomed over her, hissing venom.

"I am mistress here, and you have no rights. I knew you were trouble, oh, I knew. What do you call this?"

She swung away to the bed, grabbed one of the garments off it, and shook it in Isolde's face.

"My breeches!"

"Your breeches? Yours?" Another garment was seized and thrust towards Isolde. "And I suppose this is your jacket too?"

Using the clothes, she leaned in and beat them about Isolde, screaming as she did so.

"Hoyden! Brass-faced little hussy! How dare you bring your disgusting, wanton habits into this house?"

Isolde rolled on her side, bringing up her arms to protect her head as the foul names drove in the blows.

"Slut! Filth! Trollop!"

The attack ceased after a moment and Isolde drew sobbing breaths as she cautiously raised her head. The woman was no longer standing over her.

Flinging across the room, Alicia was now tugging on the bell-pull with unnecessary vigour. Then she swept back to the bed and gathered the rest of the clothes there, turning with them bundled up in her hands and holding them away from her as if they were contaminated.

"You'll not wear these again, I'll see to that."

The threat to her precious boy's clothes roused Isolde as nothing else could. She needed them!

Gathering strength and courage and ignoring her various hurts, she pushed herself off the floor and stood, swaying a little as her head dizzied from the late attack. Then she leapt for Alicia and seized the bundle, trying to pull it away.

"Give them to me!"

A heavy kick landed against her shin, a little protected by her petticoats. Isolde did not let go, although Alicia was tugging in the other direction as hard as she pulled.

"You're not getting them back. They're going on the fire!"

"Noooo!"

Without warning, Alicia let go and Isolde staggered back. Two hands landed on her shoulders and shoved. Down Isolde went again, losing her grip on the clothes as instinct kicked in and she tried to save herself.

The impact was severe, knocking the breath from her body. By the time she had pulled herself together and was making to rise, Alicia had gathered up the clothes and Becky was in the room.

"Lord-a-mussy!"

It was the only exclamation she had time to make, for Alicia rushed at her.

"Take these, girl! Get them to the kitchens and burn them. Throw them in the fire!"

Isolde screamed a protest and pushed to her feet even as Alicia shoved Becky towards the door.

"Get going! Get out, girl, before I give you the back of my hand!"

Becky's terrified eyes swirled towards Isolde and she hesitated. Alicia slapped her. The girl let out a cry and ran to the door.

Isolde saw her male attire disappearing through the aperture and a black rage consumed her. Flying at Alicia, she battered her with her fists, driving her against the wall. "You heartless creature! Wicked! I hate you, I hate you!"

For a moment, Isolde felt powerful and strong. But a hand shot out, her ear was seized and twisted, and a fresh piercing pain made her squeal in distress. Her fists dropped a little and her opponent took instant advantage.

Isolde could not count the blows. Her head swam, her ears were ringing. Already battered and bruised, she had little strength left to retaliate. She tried, her fingers clawing in a bid to scratch at the other's face.

A hand forced her head down and her hair was seized. Isolde felt as if it would come out by the roots as Alicia dragged her from the room by the hair, tearing down the corridor so that she stumbled and crashed along behind.

Disoriented and in agony, Isolde could only endure as the creature hauled her along to the accompaniment of a fresh deluge of insults which she no longer heard distinctly. In the background of her tortured mind, a murmur of voices started up. A flicker of thought gave a tiny hope of rescue, but no one intervened.

At last the hideous ordeal came to an end. Alicia stopped and the agonizing pull at her scalp eased, slight enough to afford a modicum of release, though she was still held with her head down, taking in the chequered floor beneath.

"Open the door!"

"If I may point out, madam —" The butler's austere tones, calm as ever. He was cut off.

"You may not. Open the door, I said."

A blast of cold air told Isolde that this command had been obeyed. Her mind leapt into gear. Alicia was going to throw her out of the house!

"Madam, I beg you to notice the state of the weather."

"Be quiet, Topham! Don't interfere."

A new voice was heard. "Miss de Baudresey, have you thought of his lordship?"

Mrs Pennyfather? Isolde put up her hands to her hair, trying to pull it from Alicia's grasp. She received a clout across the ear for her pains. Protests rose on two sides.

"Madam!"

"His lordship will scarcely approve, madam."

"I'll handle his lordship. You will none of you interfere, if you value your place. One word more, and you may expect to be dismissed without a character."

Silence.

Isolde gathered her courage. She was not giving in without a fight. "Let me go!"

"I'm going to let you go," came the snarled response. "Right this minute."

The grasp on her hair miraculously released, and Isolde let out a gasp of relief, struggling to come upright. She caught a glimpse of the butler's face, taut but expressionless. She could see only the dark gown of the housekeeper. And then a hand was in the small of her back and she was propelled over the threshold and onto the cold stone porch.

"Get out and stay out! Never let me see your face again!"

Isolde managed to turn as the great door swung back and clanged shut.

Chapter Sixteen

Dazed and aching, Isolde stared at the closed door. This could not be happening. Even Alicia could not mean to leave her outside in the freezing cold. The thought brought awareness and she realised she had not even the shawl she had gone to fetch. Cold was already penetrating her thin woollen gown, superseding the dulling pains of her various bruises.

Panic overtook her, and she rushed to the door, battering on the wood.

"Let me in! Let me in! I swear I will never do anything you don't like. Alicia, please let me in!"

No answer. Nothing. No sound, no response. Yet Isolde was sure the woman was standing on the other side of the door. Was this meant to torture her? Surely she would eventually open the door. She could not truly mean to leave her out here. She had nothing to keep her warm.

Realisation hit. No warmth, no shelter, no food or drink. Though that mattered little because she would die of the cold before she could starve to death.

Desperate, she ran to the bell and pulled at it, sending peals ringing through the house. She dragged it down again and again, making such a cacophony that the entire household must hear it.

She stopped, waiting. The door remained obstinately shut.

Her mind began to daze with disbelief. She cupped her hands and shouted.

"At least let me get my things! Alicia! Alicia!"

Nothing. Silence.

Isolde's chest heaved and sobs rose up in her chest as she stared at the black expanse of the wooden door. Her mind blanked. She could not think beyond the fact that she was out here, on her own, in the perishing cold.

Deep down, the beginnings of terror lurked. She was alone, defenceless and she was going to die. A whisper trembled on her breath. "Richard…"

An echo of his image crept into her head, and as if she would look for him, she turned from the house and trod heavily down the icy stairs. Feeling and thought began to numb, and her aimless steps carried her away from the house.

"Miss Izzy! Miss Izzy!"

The throaty whisper came at her from somewhere close at hand. Only partially aware, Isolde paid no attention.

"Miss Izzy!"

Louder now. Isolde halted and looked about.

"No, don't stop. Keep walking. She's watching from the window."

Obediently, without quite realising what she did, Isolde began to move again. She had no notion where the voice was coming from, and though she looked to left and right she saw only the bushes and trees that lined the drive.

"Go on, Miss Izzy. Round the next bend. Then we'll be out of sight of the house."

Her mind began slowly to work again. Vaguely she recalled, from her arrival, the winding journey from the entrance gates. It had seemed a long way then. Now it took an eternity. Time had slowed to a meaningless point of nothingness.

The voice exhorted her to keep walking. Not far now. Isolde obeyed. There was nothing else to do.

"There, that'll do, miss. She won't see nothing now."

Isolde stopped, looking for the source of the voice. Then Becky came running out from behind the trees. She was carrying something. Next moment, Isolde was wrapped in a rough woollen cloak, and Becky's arm came about her, holding her close. The maid was young, but she was sturdy and Isolde immediately felt supported.

"There now, that's better, isn't it, Miss Izzy?"

Isolde looked at her. "Thank you, Becky. The cloak will help a lot."

Becky clicked her tongue. "She's a mean piece, that madam. Just wait 'til his lordship hears about this. He'll give her pepper, he will."

What good would that do? Isolde did not try to make sense of it. She smiled at the maid. "Thank you, Becky. You'd best go back. She'll dismiss you if she finds out."

The maid's eyes widened, and she laughed. "Bless you, Miss Izzy, did you think I were going to let you go off alone?"

Puzzlement wreathed Isolde's mind. With the cloak around her, the numbness was going and she was beginning to feel the cold again.

"You can't come with me, Becky. I can't even support myself."

Another laugh escaped the girl. "Why, miss, it's muddled you are and no mistake. Mrs P sent me to fetch you back to the house."

"What? But —"

"Oh, don't worrit yourself, Miss Izzy. We'll keep you hidden like. Come on, let's get you inside before you catch your death."

The thought of being inside was enough to give Isolde the impetus to move. Although her hurts were beginning to make themselves felt again and she was shivering with cold. "I'm sorry, Becky, I'm a bit slow."

"After the battering she give you, miss, I'm not surprised. Mrs P and Mr Topham was that mad when I told them."

"You saw it?"

"I saw as you'd been thumped good, Miss Izzy, the moment I came into the room. And I didn't go to the kitchen like she told me. I waited and watched, I were that worrited for you. And I saw what she did and all."

Isolde's eyes misted. "Becky, you're a true friend."

The maid hurried her along, flitting along an unknown path through the trees at the edge of the grounds. "I don't know about that, miss, but let that wretch do what she did and stand by I couldn't, not if I was to be pilloried for it. Why, she might as well have killed you outright."

She talked on in this strain as she guided Isolde to an outhouse at the back of Bawdsey Manor. It looked to be some kind of store, for it was full of old furniture stacked around the walls. There were two high windows, no carpet, and no fireplace, yet Isolde immediately felt a degree warmer for the presence of walls.

"We're behind the stables, Miss Izzy. We'll get a brazier in here soon as ever we can. But sit you down now and I'll fetch Mrs P."

Isolde was pushed into an old deep chair, its upholstered seat and leather back split, the stuffing coming out. She was glad enough to sit down. Becky bade her rest and scuttled off. She sat back in the chair, huddling into the cloak and let her head fall back. A deep sigh escaped her, and tears of relief seeped from her eyes.

The argument was long and wearing. First Mrs Pennyfather did her best to dissuade Isolde. When that failed, she brought in the butler to try and make her see reason. Only Becky understood, but she kept mum before her seniors, conveying her thoughts by a series of grimaces and eye rolling behind the butler's back.

"You have only to wait until his lordship returns, Miss Cavanagh. I have no doubt he will take your part."

"Yes, but then what?" argued Isolde. "He won't remain with me all the time. At some point, Miss de Baudresey will catch me alone and I shall be at her mercy."

Mrs Pennyfather clicked her tongue. "You'll tell his lordship everything, Miss Cavanagh, and he will act appropriately."

"How? Short of locking her up, what can he do?"

The butler and housekeeper exchanged a glance, but neither answered this directly. Mrs Pennyfather turned back to Isolde. "If you will not think of yourself, pray think of us. What do you suppose his lordship will say if we allow you to go off alone?"

"I'll leave a letter for him saying I wouldn't listen to you."

The butler shook his head. "I fear that will not answer, Miss Cavanagh. His lordship is your official guardian. You are bound by law to adhere to his wishes."

"In that case, perhaps you'd have me go back in to Miss de Baudresey and ask her to resume teaching me how to be a lady."

The elderly servants eyed her in frowning silence. Isolde knew she was putting them in a difficult position, but they were not privy to the whole story. They did not know about Lord Vansittart, nor that Richard had pledged himself to make contact with him on her behalf, at some point. If she could reach her uncle, she might find out for herself whether she had an alternative refuge, which had become imperative now that Alicia had shown how far she would go.

There was no future for her here at Bawdsey Manor. Whatever response Richard made to his sister's action, her right to his support was far greater than Isolde's. He would scarcely act against his flesh and blood. Far more likely he would see the wisdom of shifting Isolde into the care of Lord Vansittart, realising that she and Alicia could never inhabit the same house.

She had rather take matters into her own hands than await an outcome she foresaw must be inevitable. Yet perhaps discretion was called for here. She sighed.

"Well, let me think about it for a while."

"A couple of days can make no difference," said Mrs Pennyfather.

"And his lordship may be back in that time," added Topham.

A remark that caused Isolde to take a resolve to be gone within the day. She made no move to dissuade the housekeeper from ordering a truckle bed to be set up for her in the store room and directing Becky to bring sheets, blankets and a couple of quilts. A brazier had already been brought, giving off both smoke and heat, and Mrs Pennyfather produced a basket of provisions to keep hunger at bay. She left, promising to return with salves and unguents to anoint Isolde's various hurts.

"When the bed's made, Miss Cavanagh, I'll have Becky bring you hot water and a basin for a wash. Then we'll see better what's what with your injuries."

"Thank you, Mrs Pennyfather. I will ask her for some spare clothing too, if I may."

The housekeeper consented to this, and Isolde breathed more easily. At least Becky could go into her bedchamber without incurring the housekeeper's displeasure.

"I'll get a screen in here as well." Mrs Pennyfather looked around the store room and sniffed. "It's not what I'd choose for you, but it's the safest place for the moment. The mistress would never think to look for you here, even should she come to know that you didn't leave the premises."

When she and the butler had departed, Isolde waited for Becky to return with the bedlinen, revolving plans in her head. James the footman arrived with the truckle bed and set it up, grinning cheerfully at her the while.

"You look like a bruiser in the ring, miss, if you don't mind me saying so."

Isolde put up a hand to feel her face. Every part of it was tender and there was scarcely any part of her body that did not produce discomfort as she moved. Nevertheless, she smiled at James.

"Perhaps Miss de Baudresey should think of a career in that line."

He let out a laugh. "I can just see her, miss. She'd have them betting the odds in her favour in no time."

When he'd gone, Isolde sank back into her chair, setting her elbow on the arm and, somewhat gingerly, leaning her cheek into her cupped hand. Part of her plan was going to be easy enough. She already had provisions to carry with her, so that was not a problem. But how in the world was she to get from here to Hertfordshire in this severe weather?

The solution crept into her mind and she caught her breath. Dared she? It was one thing to walk away from Richard's protection. Quite another to steal one of his horses.

But, she argued to herself, it was not really stealing. She would return it once she was done. She was only borrowing it, and surely Richard would not begrudge her this one small favour after what his sister had done to her?

Should she leave a message for him, after all? Although she had said as much to the upper servants, that had been only to placate them. It would defeat her purpose to write to Richard. He must not know what she intended, or where she had gone, until she'd had a chance to confront Lord Vansittart herself.

A twinge of conscience threatened to ruin her scheme, but she hardened her heart. This was her life. Richard had accepted her with a good grace, but there could be no doubt she was a problem to him. He had not wanted her in the first place, even if in the last he had shown himself sympathetic. He'd gathered her into his embrace — where she would very much like to be at this moment — and let her cry into his coat.

Isolde felt tightness grow in her chest, making her breath short.

She must not think of that. He was only being kind, and kindness would not serve to protect her from Alicia's vengeance. The unacknowledged hope she'd harboured was irrational and she was glad she had succeeded in quashing it before Alicia attacked her. Now she could go on her way without regret. She hoped.

Before she could drive herself into a quagmire of contradictory thoughts, Becky reappeared with an enormous armload of bedlinen. Puffing, she pushed her way into the store room and dumped the lot on the bed. Isolde half rose from her seat, but the maid waved her down.

"Don't you fret, Miss Izzy, I can manage. I've a surprise for you, too."

"A surprise?"

The maid's cheeks were bright with effort, and she was out of breath, but she grinned. Bending over the pile she'd brought, she lifted a corner and, like a conjuror flourishing his cloth, she turned it aside, disclosing a familiar-looking pile of bunched-up clothing.

"I hid them, miss. As if I'd have burned them, no matter what she said!"

Enlightenment dawned, and Isolde uttered a shriek, jumping to her feet. She regretted the hasty motion at once as her battered body protested, but she paid no heed, crossing quickly to the truckle bed.

"My boy's clothes! Oh, Becky, thank you. I was going to ask you to find me some male attire, even if you had to steal it from one of the menservants."

"They're that crumpled, Miss Izzy," said Becky as Isolde sifted through the garments, checking everything was there, "but I can soon set that to rights. I'll bring in the iron and they'll be good as new."

"Becky, you are an angel. I can't thank you enough."

"Is all there, miss? What else do you need?"

Isolde paused, looking across at the maid. Had she guessed? Becky's brows rose and she tutted.

"You didn't think as how I didn't know you meant to go anyhow, Miss Izzy?"

"I should have realised you would. The shirt is here, but there's a cravat missing, and some small clothes. Oh, and stockings. My boots and hat too. They're at the bottom of the trunk, if Alicia hasn't emptied it."

"She's not done that, miss. She's not been next or nigh your chamber yet, though Janey told me she said as how she meant to be rid of everything."

Isolde's guts clenched. "Then there is no time to lose!"

She gave Becky exact instructions and the girl nodded and hurried away. She would eat and sleep tonight as best she could, and wake early in the morning. She was used to early rising, but she'd ask Becky to call her as soon as she got up, just in case.

In the event, she was already up and dressed with her provisions packed by the time Becky came creeping into the store room. She was stiff and sore, but the salves Mrs Pennyfather had used on her had helped her sleep in relative ease. It was going to be an uncomfortable ride, but that could not be helped.

It was pitch dark in the room, but the maid had brought an oil lamp and she guided Isolde to the stables. The grooms were not yet up, though they would no doubt appear in short order.

Isolde found a saddle and tackle without difficulty, but choosing a horse was another matter. She went from stall to stall, softly greeting each occupant until she found one that looked to be a good weight for her. A bay mare, as far as Isolde could tell. The horse whickered in response to her blandishments, answering with a friendly toss of the head.

Isolde talked the mare into quiet and led it from the stall. She was happy enough to take the saddle and made no objection to the bit. Isolde hoped this augured well for the coming ride. She fastened the girths and strapped on saddlebags. Thanks to Becky, who had willingly dug into the bottom of her trunk, she was armed. Her father's sword was soon strapped onto one bag, her pistol and provisions tucked into the other.

All of a sudden Becky grabbed Isolde's wrist. Were the stable boys coming?

"What is it?"

"I've just had a thought, miss. Have you money?"

Isolde laughed. "Have no fear. Coins are sewn into my breeches and jacket."

"Lord-a-mussy, and the mistress would've burned it all!"

"Yes, but I have other hiding places, Becky."

She was not going to give away the cunning contrivance that concealed the bulk of her funds in one of her boots. Reassured, Becky held the bridle and Isolde mounted up. She settled herself in the saddle and arranged the thick cloak to give as much protection as possible from the cold. She felt the horse's mouth and urged her gently out of the stable block. She cast a glance around the yard, but it was still free of servants.

"You'd best ride around the edge of the forest, Miss Izzy. You'll be seen if you go down the drive."

Isolde thanked her and leaned down from the saddle to clasp the maid's hand. "You've done so much, Becky. I won't forget."

"Good luck, miss. Be careful."

Isolde nodded and clicked her tongue at the mare. It was many weeks since she'd been on horseback, and her misused body was protesting. But she'd been well taught and she was used to riding astride. She looked at Becky, touched her whip hand to the brim of her hat in salute, and set off.

She could not help smiling to herself. Lord Vansittart was in for a surprise.

Chapter Seventeen

The freezing weather persisted and the inside of the carriage felt cold and damp. Richard wished he was driving his curricle. At least he would have enough to do in controlling his team, which would have kept his mind off his discomfort — and those uncomfortable thoughts that had plagued him from the moment he left Bawdsey Grange.

All through the affairs that occupied him in settling the aftermath of his mother's death, the niggle in his head would not be banished. Now, with all too much leisure for thought, the niggle had become a plague.

Try as he would, he had not been able to get Isolde's face out of his mind. Those damned expressive eyes! Her voice echoed in his head, and he found himself regretting every harsh word he had ever spoken to her. He could only be glad he'd left her in kindness, although the remembrance of Alicia's strange look still troubled him. He could only hope his fears were mistaken.

His conscience smote him still for that cursed night he'd snapped at her. And the remembrance of her tear-stained cheeks when she came to find a book in the library would haunt him forever. He remembered how he had been conscious of her presence the whole time, unable to concentrate on the business he'd had in hand. So many letters, so much to do. And he'd left it until the last minute to allay the poor child's distress. It was unworthy. She might have chosen her time badly, but she was clearly in a great deal of alarm for her future. He should have paid more attention, taken the time to talk her into calm again.

Still, with matters more settled, he might take leisure to turn his attention to her difficulties. What he would tell her of Vansittart he could not decide. What he did know was that he could not in conscience hand Isolde over to her uncle. The man was ruthless, and would only want the girl if he could turn her to his advantage. Better to keep her away from him altogether.

Which left her squarely on his hands. Fortunately she was young yet, and there was time in which to prepare her for society. Here Richard's mind balked. The correct procedure was to take the girl to London for a season and find her a suitable husband. Somehow this course was distinctly unpalatable. Besides, it was fraught with difficulty. Even could she cope with the complexities of that social whirl, how in the world could he introduce her without revealing her relationship to Vansittart? The man would be bound to cause trouble, if only to coerce him into paying down his dust for this accursed cotton plantation.

It was hard to imagine what sort of man would be willing to take a child brought up more boy than girl, with no portion to recommend her. Although any man who knew her must readily discover attributes that had no bearing on her social eligibility. The touching naivety that was counterbalanced by a boldness born of bravado. The warm heart with its impulse of sympathy, even if the manner of it was misplaced. How many debutantes were as quick, or as bright? Indeed, unspoiled by arts and artifice in a way that could not but enchant the male breast.

No, there could surely be no difficulty in marrying her off. Which was the only possible future for her. Isolde might blithely speak of finding employment, but that was ineligible on all counts. She was granddaughter to an earl, for one thing.

For another, she couldn't do anything of the least use in the only occupations available to genteel females.

He had discussed as much with Mama, who had, he recalled, been amused by the girl's determination to support herself somehow. But his mother had known as well as he how impossible that was. Nor could he have rested easy, knowing Isolde was out there somewhere, working her fingers to the bone. No, it would not do.

He had made himself responsible for her, and he must take the consequences. It was, in effect, no worse than having Alicia on his hands. A deal better, to be truthful. Passing an evening in Isolde's company, rather than his sister's, could only be a significant improvement. And he must get her off his hands before he married himself, as he must one day if his title and lands were not to pass to a remote cousin. What woman could be expected to endure a household containing an older woman determined to rule the roost, and a youthful bundle of mischief with no prospects?

He dwelled with pleasure on the memory of discovering Isolde wielding one of the foils in his gun-room. She was an original, no doubt of that. If only she might be permitted to be herself, without the shibboleths governing the female of the species, she would undoubtedly thrive and delight all who came in contact with her. That, however, was quite out of the question.

Richard sighed, conscious of a sense of dissatisfaction for which he could not account. He tried to banish thought and composed himself for sleep, succeeding in dropping off for a while to the rhythmic swaying of the carriage. His dreams were nebulous, but disturbing, and he woke with a feeling of urgency to be home, the piquant face of his dreams shifting effortlessly into his waking mind.

As the carriage turned in at the gates, Richard's blood quickened inexplicably. He had no thought in his head of anything beyond anticipation of how Isolde might greet him.

The coach stopped, the door was opened, the steps let down. Mechanically, Richard descended and walked up the stone stairs to the open door where his butler was waiting to receive him. He allowed himself to be divested of his hat, gloves and great-coat.

"Is all well, Topham?"

The man did not reply, busying himself with the garments. Richard thought nothing of it. Perhaps the fellow had not heard him. He had been in service here since before Richard was born and might well be growing deaf.

Having handed the clothes to James and the valet Fareham, who had come hurrying down the stairs, Topham gave his master a bow and gestured to the dining-parlour.

"Dinner will be served within a half hour, my lord, unless you wish for more time to remove the travel stains?"

"No, thank you. Half an hour will suffice."

He must suppose the ladies were changing for dinner, for it was unlike Alicia not to come into the hall to welcome him. She made a point of ensuring her position as the mistress of house was never overlooked, Richard remembered, a trace of cynicism in the thought.

He made haste with his toilet, changing his travelling clothes for the black silk breeches and coat more suited to the table and walked directly to the dining-room. The family had got out of the way of foregathering in the drawing-room since his mother stopped coming downstairs for dinner, except when they had guests. A rare event these last couple of years.

Alicia was already seated and she greeted him with, he thought, a trifle of reserve.

"You made good time, Richard. I hardly knew when to expect you."

He took his seat at the head of the table. "It hardly seemed worth sending an express. I could not suppose it to be necessary."

"Not in the least," she agreed, signing to the butler to begin serving.

Richard glanced at the door, expecting at any moment to see it open to admit the slim form of Isolde, slipping into the room in that unobtrusive way she had. "Should we not wait for Isolde?"

"No need."

It was curtly said, and Richard glanced at his sister. Had matters not improved between them? He knew Alicia was inclined to despise the girl, but he'd hoped she might at least have heeded his admonitions to take care of Isolde.

Topham was filling his glass with ruby liquid. Glancing up to thank him, Richard noted tautness in the austere features. Was the man avoiding his eye?

He was on the point of enquiring into this when James appeared, ready to serve him with some sort of fricassee. To his astonishment, as he laid a portion meticulously on the plate, the footman caught his eye and wiggled his eyebrows.

What in the world was that about? Had the fellow been drinking? He looked down the table to where James was laying down the dish and taking up another upon which reposed a cut pigeon pie. Richard watched him move around to serve Alicia. When he had done so, again he raised his eyes to Richard's. A discreet cough from Topham and the footman was once more the invisible servant, serving him without expression.

Richard looked at the empty place across from Alicia. All at once, the anomalies coalesced into a cutting shaft as a presentiment shot through him. He turned to his sister. "Where is Isolde?"

For an instant, she kept her eyes upon her plate. They rose, flashing with contempt.

"She left."

"What?"

"I'm afraid she left us, brother."

Richard's mind blanked. "Left us? What do you mean, she left us?"

Her lip curled. "What do you think I mean? She has gone."

"Gone where?"

"How in the world would I know? She slipped away. Nothing was said of her intentions."

Bewilderment was beginning to give way to anger, and a stirring of apprehension.

"And you let her go?"

Alicia was glaring at him. Her voice came low and vibrant, throbbing with emotion. "Let her? There was no question of letting her go." She drew a breath and let it out with violence. "If you must have it, I threw her out."

Richard could not speak. A maelstrom crowded his mind. The oddity of the behaviour of his servants jumbled with images of Isolde, a desire to strangle his sister, and a tearing fear of what could have become of the child.

Alicia was not yet done. "What would you? The girl offered me violence. She is a hoyden, little better than a strumpet. Do you know what I found in her trunk? A set of male clothing, if you will believe me. Would you expect me to house any such? No, indeed, brother, she can have no home here. I flung her from the premises, with nothing but the clothes she stood up in."

The words battered at Richard's brain, but this last loosened his tongue. He rose in his wrath, oblivious to the presence of the servants. "Have you taken leave of your senses?"

"Not I, brother."

"Dear Lord in heaven, what did you think you were doing? I would not treat a dog in such a fashion!"

His sister was on her feet, her hands grasping the edge of the table, words panting from her lips. "No! You are blind and a fool. Could you not see what she would be at? Had you no eyes to recognise the scheming little hussy for what she is? Oh, such innocent eyes! Oh, such a winning manner! She even had my mother eating out of her hand. But not me, brother, not me. I knew what she was from the first. Believe me, you are well rid of her."

Richard stared at her, beset by so many conflicting emotions he could not think straight. The one thing that stood out above all others was that his sister was indeed beyond reason. He'd always known her for a jealous woman, grudging contentment to any in her vicinity, worse since her humiliation at the altar. But he feared now she was truly unhinged.

He flung down his napkin, struggling to command his temper. "You have committed a grave wrong, Alicia. I only pray I will be able to undo whatever harm you may have done." Turning away from her, he threw a furious glance at his butler as he strode from the dining parlour. "Topham, come with me!"

"How could you let this happen? How could the two of you stand by and permit your mistress to commit such a villainous act?"

Reaching his library, Richard had made straight for the decanters, poured himself a measure of brandy and tossed it off. He was in control again, able to operate in at least a semblance of his usual manner as he addressed the senior servants before him.

Mrs Pennyfather, fetched at his command by the butler, looked worn and dismayed, but she spoke with all her usual coherence. "My lord, we could not interfere in sight of the mistress, for she threatened us with dismissal."

Richard snorted. "Don't be ridiculous. My sister has no authority to dismiss either of you from this house, or indeed any servant of mine. You should have known that."

Topham intervened. "Discretion, my lord, seemed the better part of valour. The mistress was beside herself with rage. Had we interfered —"

"I don't care if she threw herself to the floor and drummed her heels in a fit of hysterics. What I object to is that you allowed Miss Cavanagh to be ejected from the house in such a high-handed fashion and did nothing."

"But we did, my lord. We sent to succour her immediately, but in secret," pleaded the housekeeper, distressed.

A faint trickle of relief crept into the hideous visions of disaster that were clouding Richard's mind. "You brought her back?"

"Yes, my lord, of course we brought her back."

He let his breath go in a long sigh. "Thank God! Where is she?"

Mrs Pennyfather's eyes sought the butler's and they exchanged an agonised glance that had the immediate effect of reviving Richard's fears.

"For God's sake, speak out, will you?"

Topham's disapproving expression overspread his features and he looked decidedly reproachful. "If you will allow us to speak, my lord, I believe you will not be dissatisfied."

Richard drew an impatient breath, but held his peace, merely nodding at the man to continue.

"Mrs Pennyfather sent young Becky after Miss Cavanagh with a cloak to cover her. She went through the trees so the mistress would not see her, for Miss Alicia was watching from the window as Miss Cavanagh went down the drive. Becky brought her back."

"And we put her in the store room behind the stables, my lord," said the housekeeper, taking up the tale. "I caused a truckle bed to be made up, and we put a brazier in there and brought provisions. Later, I anointed her hurts."

He had listened to the unfolding story in mounting dismay, tempered by relief that his servants had the sense to secure Isolde and keep her hidden from Alicia. But at these words, shock seized him. "Hurts?"

Again the two servants exchanged a glance. The butler took the question.

"Miss Cavanagh had the misfortune to be injured during the altercation."

He eyed them both, suspicion and doubt in his head. They were keeping something from him. He sharpened his tone. "Well? Out with it! Don't attempt to deceive me, I beg."

Mrs Pennyfather gripped her hands tightly together. "My lord, we did our best. But Miss Cavanagh slipped away in the early morning."

For one hideous moment, Richard thought she meant Isolde had died. His tongue froze.

"She took the bay mare, my lord," said the butler.

The whoosh of relief was superseded by a new fear. "She rode? Without a groom? Without money, without protection? Have either of you any idea where she has gone?"

"None, my lord." Then the housekeeper brightened. "But Becky might know something. She swears she has no idea where Miss Cavanagh has gone. I questioned her closely, my lord, but she could tell me nothing more than I already knew. Only…"

The hesitation sent a flicker of hope into Richard's breast.

"Only what, Mrs Pennyfather?"

A little sigh escaped the woman. "Well, it's likely nothing, but young Janey let it out that Miss Cavanagh had made quite a friend of Becky. The girl denies it, but —"

"Fetch her here to me at once."

Mrs Pennyfather left the room and Topham went to retrieve the decanter. Richard sank into his favourite armchair by the fire, prey to unreasoning panic somewhere deep inside which he strove to control. The butler refilled his glass and brought it over, and Richard found some comfort in the burn of the fiery spirit down his throat.

"If you will excuse me for a moment, my lord, I will instruct James to have the dinner dishes returned to the kitchen to be rewarmed. I think you should eat something, my lord."

"Thank you, but I have no appetite."

A disapproving frown was bent upon him. "If you will forgive me saying so, my lord, it will not help matters to starve yourself."

Richard flung up a hand. "Very well. But not until I have sifted this matter of Miss Cavanagh's present whereabouts."

"Even if you are able to, my lord, you will scarcely set out after her tonight. In such weather as this, you cannot hope to come up with her in the dark."

Although everything in him urged Richard to leap instantly into action, he was obliged to acknowledge the truth of this. Indeed, it would in all probability do more harm than good, since he was likely to run into difficulties himself. Nevertheless, regardless of what the maid was able to add, he would start out in search of Isolde in the morning.

When Topham returned, he instructed him to prime Reeve to be ready with the curricle at an early hour, and turned with eagerness as the housekeeper reappeared with one of the young maids in tow. Richard rose and went to meet the girl.

"Ah, Becky, I am in need of your help," he said, attempting a soft approach. There was little point in frightening the girl with a show of authority.

To his surprise, the maid met his glance with a degree of belligerence in both face and pose.

"Yes, my lord?"

"You tended Miss Cavanagh, I understand."

"Not exactly, my lord. Only she were kind to me and — and she'd talk to me a bit."

The words were subservient enough, but the tone was not, although the girl threw a brief glance towards the two senior servants standing to one side.

Richard was tempted to dispense with their presence, but he knew it would be an unforgiveable breach of protocol. Not that he cared much for that at this particular moment, but it would serve no good purpose to distress his servants. And they had done what they might for Isolde. He dredged up an encouraging smile.

"I am glad Miss Cavanagh had someone she could talk to. But you see, Becky, she is a lady and she has gone off without protection, and I must find her as quickly as I can."

To his mingled surprise and irritation, the maid's eyes danced.

"Oh, she's not in any danger, my lord, not Miss Izzy."

"How so?"

Again, she glanced at the upper servants, way above her in the hierarchy, and Richard intervened. "I will engage for it that nothing you tell me will get you into trouble, Becky. This is far too important to be holding anything back. If you can tell me where she went, I will be eternally in your debt."

A dismayed frown crept over the girl's face. "But I can't, my lord. I don't know. She didn't tell me, honest. Only she said as how she couldn't stay, and I knew she wouldn't, not after the way the mistress —"

She broke off, hands flying to her mouth and with another look towards Mrs Pennyfather, this time of clear apprehension.

Richard was having none of it. He sharpened his tone. "After the way the mistress what, Becky? Be open with me!"

The girl seemed to struggle with herself for a moment, but it was plain that a well of indignation would not be contained, for out it came in a rush. "Oh, sir, you should have seen it! The mistress didn't half slap her to pieces. Blows and blows she give her, and poor Miss Izzy fell to the ground. She got up again and tried to give as good as she got, but she were dazed, for I were peeping through the doorway, though the mistress had sent me off with the clothes. She told me to burn them, but I never did, nor I wouldn't have if she'd beat me for it, which she did and all, though not as bad as poor Miss Izzy. I hid them, my lord, and later I took them for Miss Izzy, for I knew as she meant to go, and how better than if she were dressed like a boy?"

"What did you say?" cried the housekeeper. "Dressed like a boy? Well, I never did!"

Struggling to unravel the hideous chain of events related by the maid, and fighting to remain calm as the images presented for his inspection harrowed his mind and heart, Richard waved Mrs Pennyfather to silence. "Go on, Becky."

"Well, my lord, the upshot of it were as the mistress grabbed poor Miss Izzy by the hair, and dragged her all along the corridor, she did, shouting fit to bust herself and poor Miss Izzy crying with pain, for there weren't nothing she could do but follow after for the mistress run down that corridor like a mad thing. I crept after, and I saw as Mrs Pennyfather and Mr Topham tried to stop it, only the mistress shouted at them and all, and she chucked poor Miss Izzy out into the cold. She were only wearing a woollen gown. And I heard her crying and begging to be let in, and she rung the bell and knocked the door. And the mistress wouldn't let nobody open it, she wouldn't. Oh, my lord, it were enough to give a body nightmares!"

Aghast, Richard could only stare at the girl. Had his sister indeed run mad? Dear Lord in heaven, she ought to be confined! What he was to do with the woman, the Lord only knew.

But that was for the future. The vital thing was to find Isolde and bring her back. He remembered the maid's first words.

"You said she was not in any danger. What made you say that?"

Becky tossed her head. "For as I fetched her pistol and a sword she said as belonged to her Pa, and she took them both with her."

Both upper servants exclaimed at this, but Richard paid no heed.

"Had she any money?"

"Yes, my lord, she said she had it somewhere secret like."

A modicum of the deep-seated panic that had been riding Richard began to subside. The situation might not be as dire as he had supposed. If she could pass muster as a boy, and she was armed — with weapons she'd assured him she knew how to use — she stood a chance for at least a day or two. That she was equipped with funds was a Godsend. Thank heaven she'd had the sense to take his mare and ride!

Now all he had to do was follow her trail and find out where she had gone. If he could discover no trace of her, he had a shrewd notion of one place she might try to reach. The thought of the reception Isolde could find there was enough to revive all his earlier apprehension.

Chapter Eighteen

The house was visible from the gates, which were surprisingly dilapidated, rusty and worn, one of them hanging off a hinge. The building was neither as large nor as daunting as Bawdsey Grange, although it stood two stories high, square and relatively plain, with a mellow look to the walls, weathered to variegated shades of yellow, even in the dimness of a winter's day.

Isolde's courage took a leap. Perhaps she might find a welcome here after all. If Lord Vansittart was in residence. If he would consent to see her.

She'd had ample time for reflection upon the journey, rumbling along in the stagecoach from Harwich. Rejecting all too disturbing memories of Bawdsey Grange, Isolde rehearsed what she should say to her uncle. She was unable to help wishing this journey had not been necessary, but at least it would settle the matter one way or the other. She would know whether there was a refuge for her at Greville House, and could act accordingly.

It had been easy enough to discover her uncle's likely whereabouts. Enquiries at The Duke's Head in Harwich sent her to a local resident in possession of a Peerage, from which she hoped to learn where precisely in Cheshire the Vansittart estate was situated. When Isolde found he had a nearer place in Hertfordshire, she at once thought to try there first. It was much closer, a far less arduous journey. With luck, she might not be put to the trouble of travelling half across the country to find him.

Leaving the mare stabled at the inn, Isolde took the quicker route by stage, changing once in order to go cross-country to Bishop's Stortford. With funds enough to pay her way, her most pressing concern was the necessity to maintain her disguise.

A deeper voice and a manly stride worked in her favour, though it was useless to expect anyone to take her for better than a slight youth, not yet old enough to require the use of a razor. Her bruises caused comment and question, but she deflected them with a story of having been set upon by a thief, whom she'd vanquished with the use of her sword.

The horse she'd hired at The Cock this morning was a sturdy beast with his own sense of speed. Moreover, the innkeeper's directions to Greville House proved inadequate and she was obliged to enquire the way several times. Consequently the morning was already advanced and Isolde added hunger to the gnawing apprehension in her stomach.

Now she was here, the anxiety deepened, tempered a little by the apparent warmth of the house ahead of her. She was relieved that she had taken the precaution of slipping her pistol into the pocket of her cloak rather than dropping it into the saddlebag she had unlaced and perforce brought with her from Harwich, lacking any other receptacle for her belongings. However, she could scarcely enter her uncle's house armed with a sword. It would have to remain strapped to the saddle on the hired horse.

During the journey, she had gone over what she would say again and again, changing it all with frequency. It bore too close a resemblance to that earlier journey when she had been overtaken with the fear her named guardian would hate her. How much more likely was that expectation from Lord

Vansittart? Worse, it occurred to her for the first time that her arrival in male attire might prove excessively awkward.

Well, it was no manner of use loitering here. She dug her heels into the horse's flank and urged him through the open gates. Cantering down the drive, she took a moment to glance around the grounds. The rolling lawns were overgrown and covered in dead leaves and debris, leafless trees stood out stark in the encroaching woods and the mellow walls, as she neared, proved a deal more weathered than she had supposed.

It began to look as if Lord Vansittart could not possibly be living here, though the knocker had not been taken off the door and the shutters were open.

Reaching the small portico before the entrance, Isolde dismounted and looked in vain for somewhere to tether the horse. There was nothing for it but to lead the animal with her as she went forward to ply the knocker. Its echo resounded within and she stepped back a pace, unnerved.

Footsteps sounded in a few moments, and the door was opened a small way, a plump face in a mob cap peering around it. Relief surged through Isolde. At least she did not have to deal with a personage as intimidating as the butler Topham.

"Is Lord Vansittart at home?"

The maid took her time before replying, looking Isolde up and down and lifting her brows at sight of the horse so close to the front door. She was not as young as Becky, but it was evident she was one of the lowlier servants.

"Well," she said at last, "he is and he isn't."

Isolde tried again. "May I see him, if you please? I am here on urgent business."

A frown descended and the girl chewed her lip a moment. "I could ask. Who should I say is calling?"

Which was the crux of the matter. She could scarcely announce herself as Miss Cavanagh. Necessity jogged her mind into gear. "Tell him I have a message from his niece."

The maid's eyes popped. "His niece? He don't have no niece."

Isolde drew a breath. "In fact he does. Only he has not seen her for a very long time. She lived abroad, you see." She saw doubt and suspicion in the girl's face, and added in a placatory tone, "You could not be expected to know."

It was evident the maid was loath to believe it, but Isolde hoped she would be uncertain enough to be unwilling to take responsibility, should it prove to be the truth.

At length, she opened the door wider and stepped to one side. "You'd best come in while I go and see."

"What about the horse? He'll take cold and I hired him at The Cock in Bishop's Stortford. I should not like to take him back in a worse condition than when we set out."

The maid sniffed. "I could ask Jed to come round and take him to the stables."

"Thank you. Will you do that first, if you please? I'll wait here."

The girl was gone so long that Isolde began to chafe. Had she forgotten? Or simply changed her mind and decided not to admit her? Just as Isolde decided to knock again, a man appeared around the corner of the house, walking towards her at a leisurely pace. From his attire clearly a groom, he greeted her with a grunt and took the horse's bridle, leading him away without a word.

Moments passed. Isolde began to feel chilled, despite the woollen cloak in which she was enveloped. Becky had insisted she take it, and indeed it had been more than welcome when she was riding in the frosty winter air.

146

At last she heard footsteps and moved to the door. It opened and the same maid appeared. "His lordship says to bring you up."

Isolde's stomach clenched and her pulse kicked into life, heartbeats becoming rapid as she followed the girl into a modest hallway and up a set of stairs that wound around to the floor above, their woodwork dull and stained with sweaty finger-marks.

She was shown into a small parlour, furnished without opulence or taste. There were a couple of mismatched chairs near the fireplace, with shabby damask cushions, a filled bookcase to one side, and a small bureau in the middle, at which sat a man of middle years who did not even trouble to look up from his writing when the maid spoke.

"This is the fellow, my lord."

Leaving Isolde standing near the door, she departed, shutting the door behind her with a careless shove. As it clicked into place, Lord Vansittart lifted his head and looked across at her.

Isolde barely had time to take in the faintly silvered wings in the pale brown hair, the oddly familiar handsome face before the man's eyes sprung wide and he stared in evident shock.

"Good God!"

He had recognised her. How? Impossible to fathom, but he clearly knew. She had retained her cloak, but it hung open, revealing her clothes. His gaze slipped down and up again, and his brows lifted.

"I don't believe it!"

She swallowed. In a voice that did not seem to belong to her, she took the plunge.

"How do you do, Uncle Vere? I am Isolde Mary Cavanagh."

For several nerve-wracking moments he did not speak. His gaze travelled over her, dwelling on her bosom as if he sought to find the truth of her assertion there that she was indeed female. Astonishment died out of his face and he rose, gesturing to one of the chairs. "You'd better sit down."

Isolde moved into the room, warily regarding him. His manner was baffling. She did not know what she had expected, but not this urbane politeness.

He held out a hand. "Allow me to take your cloak."

She slipped it off and relinquished it, and removed her hat, holding it as she eyed him. He threw her cloak over the back of a straight chair by the wall and held out his hand for the hat. Without looking, he threw it in the general direction of the chair. Isolde glanced to see it fall to the floor and brought her gaze to bear on her uncle again.

Vansittart indicated the chair, a faint supercilious smile curving his lip. "Pray be seated. I won't bite, you know."

She moved to the chair and perched on its edge, watching him cross to the one opposite and settle into it, throwing one leg over the other and leaning back at his ease.

"So, Isolde Mary Cavanagh, what can I do for you?"

No clue to his thoughts was visible in his face, no matter how hard she studied him. She knew not how to begin. Out of her mouth came words for which she was quite unprepared. "You recognised me. Do you have a portrait of my mother? Am I like her?"

"You don't know? Ah no, you were a mere child when she died, as I understand it."

Quick suspicion kindled. "How do you know that?"

The brows rose, giving him a cynical look. "Cavanagh wrote to tell me so." A faint sigh escaped him. "I don't know if he hoped I might be induced to take you in then."

"No, he didn't," she returned, unable to help the snap in her voice. "Papa never expected anything from you. He didn't want me to come to you at all."

Vansittart's lip curled. "Then why are you here?"

Isolde felt the warmth rush into her cheeks and she looked quickly away. Her voice sounded gruff and resentful, even to her own ears. "I had no choice."

"Indeed?"

She drew a breath. "Did — did Richard write to you about me? I mean, Lord Alderton."

His rather hard eyes seemed to consider her. "No, he did not write to me about you."

A tiny hope flickered inside her. Had Richard intended to keep her? If he had not approached Lord Vansittart, could he have decided not to palm her off on her family? Or had he not yet made up his mind? He had not of course had much opportunity lately to do anything about her situation, which seemed the more probable reason.

There was nothing for it. She would have to tell her uncle just what had occurred. She gathered her forces. "I dare say it may seem an odd question to have asked you. You see, Papa was a great friend of Lord Alderton's father, Sir Thomas de Baudresey as he then was. When he died, he commended me to his friend's guardianship, only he didn't know Sir Thomas was already dead, and so Richard — Richard…"

She faded out, quite unable to find words to express her status regarding Richard.

"Inherited you, so to speak?"

It was said with the inflexion of suggestion, and Isolde relaxed slightly, unable to help a faint smile.

"Yes, in a way. But the truth is I have no real claim upon his guardianship, and although Lady Alderton advised me to trust him, when she died…"

"Ah, I see. When did this unfortunate event take place?"

"A fortnight since. Richard has been too busy to … and he had to go to London."

"And so you took the opportunity to escape, is that it?"

Isolde looked quickly back at him. The supercilious smile was back on his lips.

"No, it wasn't like that. Coming to you is a last resort."

His brows flew up. "I am flattered."

She felt her cheeks grow warm again and broke into hasty speech. "I didn't mean — I knew Mama's family were against the marriage. Papa told me she was cut off when they eloped. I could not suppose you would welcome me, and I would not have come if it had not been for Alicia."

"Alicia?"

"Alicia de Baudresey, Richard's sister. She threw me out."

He looked startled. "Threw you out? I am not well acquainted with Alderton, but I cannot imagine any sister of his would be so lost to all sense of what is fitting."

"She is! She's a vicious, cruel vixen and she hates me. She accused me of all kinds of things, and when she found these clothes in my trunk, she went crazy. She was going to burn them. She hit me repeatedly and then she threw me out bodily."

Vansittart's eyes roved her face. "Yes, I see now that you are a little the worse for wear. You must blame the shock of your sudden appearance. In the hubbub, I'm afraid I did not notice." He wafted a hand as if to encompass her person. "How then is it you are arrayed in this decidedly unconventional fashion? And how did you get here?"

"The servants came to my rescue. I got hold of my things, borrowed a horse and came away."

"Setting out to find me."

"Yes."

There was a pause. Lord Vansittart eyed her, and she stared back doggedly. He smiled at last, this time without a trace of the sneer that seemed to characterise him. He rose and crossed to the bell-pull. Was he going to eject her? He turned.

"I think, don't you, it might be as well to resume this discussion over refreshments. I dare say you are hungry, and I am sorely in need of a restorer. Brandy, I think, might meet the case."

The meal proved to be simple fare, consisting of a selection of cold meats, bread and cheese brought into an adjoining room which Lord Vansittart called the breakfast parlour.

"We need not stand upon ceremony. This is quite cosy, do you not think?"

Perforce, Isolde agreed to it, although she could not help a slight feeling of apprehension when the maid withdrew, the same who had answered the door and shown her up.

His lordship supplied her with slices of beef and ham, laid the cheese board within her reach and waved a languid hand at the basket of rolls and the butter dish.

Isolde ate with gusto, slowing only when she saw her uncle did not serve himself, instead making free with the contents of a decanter. She hoped he was not going to become inebriated, at least before she had a chance to broach the question of her future. Anxiety loosened her tongue. "Are you not going to eat, sir?"

"Presently."

She was disconcerted to find he continued to study her as she resumed her repast. She drank water, having refused the wine he offered, for she wished to keep her wits about her. Warmth crept into her cheeks and she was unable to keep from comment.

"Why do you stare at me so?"

A faint smile creased his lips, but Isolde noted that it did not reach his eyes.

"The resemblance is uncanny."

"Resemblance to whom?"

The supercilious curve came back to his mouth. "To me, child. There is an early portrait that might easily be you."

Shock rolled through her. Until this moment, she'd been uncertain whether or not to believe in her relationship to the man.

"My hair was redder then," he resumed, his tone musing.

"Then that is why you recognised me, even dressed like this?"

"More so." He sipped at his glass, never taking his eyes from her face. "But tell me, my dear Isolde, why such clothes?" One hand came up as she opened her mouth. "No, I don't mean at this precise moment. I can conceive that it might be safer for a lone female to travel as a boy, but it is obvious you are quite at home in them. I have no experience of the army, I admit, but I can't feel it would have gone unnoticed if this was the invariable attire of ladies who follow the drum."

Stung by the mocking tone, Isolde hit back. "You must know it isn't. But I'm not a hoyden, if that is what you suppose."

"The thought never crossed my mind."

"Well, it's what Alicia said."

Among other things, but she would not disclose the variety of unpleasant names the woman had used. Nor did she feel it incumbent upon her to explain herself to this man. Not until she knew whether he had any intention of offering her a refuge. To her relief, he did not pursue the matter, instead beginning to serve himself from the various viands spread out before them.

Without his attention on her, Isolde felt a degree less uncomfortable. She drew on her courage and took the plunge. "Would you allow me to remain here?"

His glance flew up. "Is that what you want?"

Not in the least, but it would not be politic to say so. Yet, if she could induce him to house her, even for a week or so, it would at least give her a respite to consider what she should do. She decided on bluntness. "I've nowhere else to go."

Lord Vansittart regarded her over the top of a forkful of beef. "Then it appears I have no option."

By the time the dinner hour came and went, Isolde knew little more of her uncle and family than she had on her unconventional arrival. Lord Vansittart was evidently more interested in finding out about her life than imparting anything about his, despite her questions, which he deflected with his own.

They spent the better part of the afternoon still seated at the table in the breakfast parlour, and Isolde began to wonder if he truly did mean to give her house room. Eventually, he rang the bell and, to her relief, gave instructions for her accommodation.

"Have the bed made up in the blue bedchamber. Our guest is remaining for the night."

She might have been dismayed had her uncle not explained his words as soon as the maid was out of the room.

"We will keep your identity to ourselves, my dear, until your wardrobe is replenished. Unless you have concealed your petticoats in your saddlebags?"

His mockery daunted her, but she lifted her chin. "No, sir, I have not."

He smiled, but said nothing further on the matter, instead resuming his catechism.

It did not escape Isolde's notice that he wanted to know more about the short time she'd spent at Bawdsey Grange than her years in camp, dwelling particularly on Richard's reaction to having her thrust upon him.

"Any other man might have repudiated the charge."

"Richard is not like other men."

The words were out before she could stop them. She must not allow her partiality to show. That Lord Vansittart had noticed was clear from the questioning lift to his brows. Isolde hunted her mind for a way to extricate herself and found one.

"Lady Alderton remembered me, you see. She decided Alicia should educate me for a lady. I didn't want it, but I couldn't very well refuse when she was so kind as to take me in."

The eyebrows remained aloft. "Did you not say she was ill?"

"Yes, but even so, she took time to begin my training because Alicia was in London at the time."

"Then you were largely unchaperoned, I take it?"

There was no disapproval in his face, but Isolde caught an odd note in his voice that put her on her guard. She could not identify an implication, but she was nevertheless conscious of an impulse to defend.

"It was not for long. And Lady Alderton was in the house. Besides, Richard was busy. I hardly saw him."

She recalled, belatedly, Richard's outburst when he'd realised she was related to Vansittart. He'd said the man was trying to

154

ruin him, but he had never explained that remark. Now, in her uncle's presence, Isolde felt the possibility of his being exactly the kind of man to do someone a mischief. She could not put her finger on it, but she was conscious of growing distrust.

He did not offer to show her around the house, and Isolde did not care to ask, despite a growing curiosity. Why was Lord Vansittart waited upon only by the maid? There must be a cook and she had seen a groom, but what of the rest? Had he no butler and housekeeper as at Bawdsey Grange? She tried an oblique approach. "I understood my mother came from Cheshire, sir. Don't you have a house there?"

Her uncle eyed her as he sipped at the wine he was still imbibing, the level in the bottle steadily sinking. "Have you a fancy to see my principal seat?"

"I only wondered why you were not in residence there at this time of year."

"Ah, the festive season. Vastly overrated in my view, my dear. Nothing but one long round of boredom in the company of one's neighbours."

"Don't you get lonely?"

His characteristic smile came, almost a sneer. "No longer, now that you are here, Isolde."

She forced a laugh, which sounded hollow even in her own ears. She could only hope Lord Vansittart did not notice the unreality of it. Her mistrust of him was increasing, though had she been challenged, she could not have said why.

At last, he reached for the hand bell, rang it with vigour and then pushed back his chair, rising to his feet. "I have no doubt you will wish to relax a little and remove the stains of travel. The girl will show you to your chamber."

With that, he walked out of the room and left her.

Isolde had risen, but she hesitated, wondering whether to follow. Her uncle was the strangest man. Had his interest waned? What did he expect her to do?

She went to the door and opened it upon the corridor beyond. There was no sign of his lordship, and no sign of the servant either. Isolde moved to the room where she had first encountered him and stealthily opened the door. It was empty.

She took a moment to retrieve her hat and cloak, feeling her anxiety lessen as the weight at one side of the latter recalled the pistol to her mind. Rather at a loss, she hovered in the corridor, looking first one way and then the other. The maid had still not appeared. Isolde struggled to remember which way she had taken to arrive in the small parlour. She chose correctly and came out on the landing above the stairs.

Again, she dithered. When last seen, the maid had been told to prepare a bedchamber. There seemed little point in wandering along the upper floor in search of her. She was more likely to find help below stairs. Accordingly, she ran lightly down. Her eyes swept the hall, taking in the two doors either side closest to the front door. There was another in the back panelling — the servants' quarters? — and a corridor ran off to the side opposite the stairs.

Isolde chose the nearest and pushed it open. To her surprise, the room beyond was a well-appointed saloon, done out in blue and white. There was not much furniture, but it was well polished and of matching style and there were several paintings on the walls. Untutored in the niceties of decoration she might be, but the contrast between this and the other rooms she'd seen was evident.

Intrigued, she left the place and went across the hall and through the door opposite. Shocked, she stared at the bare walls with their faded papers and the white-shrouded shapes huddled in the centre of the room. Although the shutters were open, it was plain the place was unused. It could not have seen a fire for weeks for the atmosphere was freezing.

Retreating, Isolde slid down the hall and peeped around the corner along the corridor. It was dark and dismal, and she had no desire to venture further. She was just about to take the plunge and go through the door at the back in hopes of encountering a servant, when she heard footsteps on the landing above.

Moving quickly back towards the front door, she looked up in time to see a servant girl hurrying down the stairs. This was a different maid, much younger, and dressed in the ubiquitous grey of the lesser servant.

"Oh, you must be the chambermaid."

The girl started at being addressed and, having reached the hall, bobbed a curtsy.

"Yes, sir."

For a moment, Isolde was confused. Then she remembered her attire. Of course the girl thought she was a man. She smiled. "What is your name?"

The girl blushed and dropped another curtsy. "If you please, sir, it's Aggy."

Her voice was breathy and youthful and Isolde guessed she was even younger than Becky back at Bawdsey Grange. Without thinking, she tried to put the child at ease.

"Lord Vansittart ordered the blue bedchamber to be prepared for me. I suppose that's what you've been doing?"

Again the girl flushed, and would not meet Isolde's gaze. "Yes, sir, if you please, sir."

"Perhaps you'd be kind enough to show me where it is?"

A glance was cast up at her, and Isolde saw admiration there. Belatedly recalling her disguise, she tried for a more impersonal tone, waving towards the stairs.

"After you, Aggy."

As she followed the child up the stairs, Isolde had occasion to regret her attire. She might otherwise have made a friend of the girl and pumped her for information. Perhaps with care, she could still learn something.

She waited until they reached a door situated a little way along the upstairs corridor, fortunately not in the same direction as that which led to her uncle's parlour. The girl opened it, and Isolde walked into a sizeable room, dominated by a heavy four-poster and with one large window. The walls were covered in dust-coloured paper and the bed-curtains looked to be a muddy green. Isolde could see no evidence of blue.

The maid was hovering in the doorway, plainly waiting for dismissal. Isolde sought for some means of staying her departure. "Thank you, Aggy. Before you go, can you tell me what time his lordship dines?"

"Five, if you please, sir."

The curtsies and blushes would be tiresome if Isolde was not uncomfortably aware of her own deception. Throwing caution to the winds, she took a couple of steps towards the door. "Aggy, you have no need to be shy of me. I am not what I appear."

The maid blinked at her. "Sir?"

"I'm not trying to flirt with you."

Silence. The child coloured all the more, her eyes shifting away. Isolde gave it up. In her present guise, there was no point in trying to reassure the girl. Nevertheless, she had to try for information. She opted for directness. "Where are the housekeeper and the butler?"

Surprise overspread the maid's features and for once she met Isolde's gaze. "Why, at the big house, sir, like always."

"The big house? You mean in Cheshire?"

"Yes, sir. His lordship don't keep nobbut a few of us here."

"But do you and the other maid do everything?"

"Oh no, sir, for there's Jarvis as is footman here. Only he's off today."

Which explained why the other maid was answering the bell and the door. Yet it was still odd, in comparison with what she had become accustomed to at Bawdsey Grange. Alicia's worst enemy could not have accused her of keeping an ill-run house. Stranger still was the state of the place. Everywhere bar the saloon downstairs she'd seen a lack of any sort of style.

Aggy was still waiting at the door. There did not seem much point in holding her, since she evidently knew nothing of Lord Vansittart's life in Cheshire.

The child left with alacrity upon being dismissed, and Isolde gave herself up to reflection. Inevitably, her thoughts turned to Richard.

Chapter Nineteen

Richard had not expected to find the trail so easily. Enquiries at two of the principal posting houses in Harwich yielded immediate results. Not only did the landlord of The Duke's Head remember a slim red-headed youth, but Richard's groom, baiting the horses, came seeking his master within minutes.

"The bay mare is stabled here, my lord."

For a moment, Richard thought Isolde might still be in the town, but the landlord soon put paid to that notion.

"I remember the young gentlemen, sir, for he was wishful of consulting a peerage."

"Was he indeed?" So she had decided to seek out Vansittart. "And did he find one?"

"Aye, sir. I sent him off to Mr Mallard for I know as he's got a copy, for as I've asked him many a time who's who when the nobs pass by here."

"Did he get the information he wanted?"

"I believe so, sir, for he said as he'd leave the horse here and go by the stage. And off he went, sir, the very next day."

Which meant Richard was likely no more than a day behind. And he was bound to make better time in the curricle, for Isolde may well have had to change direction, and her journey would be slow-going on the stage.

A measure of relief mitigated the anxiety that had been riding him ever since the discovery of his sister's callous conduct towards the girl. He had spoken his mind to Alicia, to no avail. She appeared incapable of rational thought where Isolde was concerned. He would not lightly forget her words when she heard of his proposed journey.

"What, brother, are you mad? You mean to go after her?"

"Of course I am going after her."

"When you are well rid of the wench? Why, I have done your business for you. You cannot have wished to have such a charge."

Richard had stared at her, as at a stranger. She seemed to have no inkling of the enormity of her conduct. He had tried reason, to little effect.

"Whether or not I wished for the charge is irrelevant, Alicia. I am responsible for the child, and her welfare is wholly my concern."

"When she is nothing to you? Nothing to our family? I do not understand you, Richard."

He had snapped at that. "And I understand you even less, Alicia. Have you no compassion? No common feeling?"

She had snorted, wholly unabashed. "For that unnatural creature? None at all. I saw through the wench from the first. A schemer, if ever I saw one."

Richard gave it up, biting his tongue on the obvious questions, for it was plain his sister was blind to reality. In what sense Isolde could be supposed to be scheming, he was unable to fathom and was obliged to dismiss the words as coming from a diseased mind.

He contented himself instead with instructing the maid Becky to pack a portmanteau with whatever Isolde might need to resume her female persona. It would not do to be travelling about the country together with Isolde in male guise. If they met anyone he knew, as a girl she would pass muster as his ward. But he could scarcely introduce her to society afterwards, if anyone was able to recognise her as the youth who'd been seen in his company at some inn or other.

In between imagining the straits into which Isolde might have got herself, Richard's mind was exercised by the problem of what in the world he was to do about his sister. He had no other thought in mind than to bring Isolde back to Bawdsey Grange, but it was plain she would not survive proximity with Alicia. Besides, he could not reconcile it with his conscience to put the child in danger of further insult and injury.

Even more dismaying to him was the intrusive thought that Isolde might wish to remain with Vansittart, assuming the fellow could be induced to offer her house room. Which was frankly unlikely, if Richard was to judge by his visit to the earl. It was all too probable he would arrive at Greville Lodge to find Isolde had received as rude a welcome there as she'd had an exit from his own home.

The thought spurred him and he found it increasingly difficult to tolerate the necessarily slower speed he was obliged to maintain in order to accommodate the inclement weather. And if Reeve was to be believed, it was likely to come on to snow again in the next four and twenty hours.

Isolde woke to cold and a grey dawn creeping in through the gaps in the bed-curtains. She was clad in her shirt and smalls, for she'd forgotten in the upset of her hasty departure to provide herself with a nightgown.

She'd slept only fitfully, for the mattress was lumpy and evidently no one had aired the sheets for some time. A pervasive smell of must tickled her nostrils and she was unable to get properly warm, despite a couple of blankets and a threadbare quilt.

Struggling out from under the covers, Isolde pushed aside the curtain, wondering what the time was. Shivering, she got out of bed and opened the shutters at the window.

The world outside was shrouded in shadow. It must still be early. Any hope of hot water for washing was vain, since the servants were likely not yet astir.

The thought of returning to the cold bed was uninviting. Isolde made do with the tepid water still in her basin from yesterday. The maidservant she'd first encountered had brought it, and Isolde recalled her uncle suggesting she might wish to wash away the travel stains.

No one had removed the bowl, nor had anyone come to take away the tray on which reposed the remains of last night's dinner.

To her mingled chagrin and surprise, Isolde had not again seen Lord Vansittart, but a tray of food had been served to her in the bedchamber. It was plain fare, but plentiful and she tucked into the slices of beef and a portion of game pie with a good appetite, washing it down with ginger ale, which was all the liquid refreshment on offer.

Dressing with alacrity, Isolde walked about the room, rubbing her arms in a bid to warm up, and hoping the chambermaid would soon arrive to make up the fire.

Was it any use ringing the bell? Or would no one be up yet? It was worth a try at least. Assuming the bell worked. There was so much wear in the house, it would come as no surprise if it did nothing at all.

Crossing to the bell-pull, she tugged it hard. She listened, but could hear no echo of a ring in the distance, despite the silence of the house.

How long she waited Isolde did not know, but it seemed like forever. She began to be hungry and wished she had left one of the two rolls that accompanied last night's meal. It might have hardened, but at least it would be something.

At length she decided she might as well go in search of the maid. Or of sustenance in the kitchen, if it came to it. At the least, she might find a room with a fire made up and get a little warmth. The breakfast parlour was the likeliest spot.

This decided, Isolde went to the door and grasped the handle. Turning it, she pulled, but the door resisted.

An exclamation of impatience escaped her. Was there nothing in the house that was not either worn or warped?

But the door continued to elude her efforts and bit by bit it dawned upon her that she was locked in.

For an uncountable time, she stared at the door, unable to think beyond the bare fact of being incarcerated. The why of it paled beside the disquieting feeling of déjà vu. Although the last time she'd been locked out instead of in. She spent fruitless moments in a bid to decide which of the two fates was worse.

When reason began to return, Isolde leapt on the conviction that her uncle must have done this. Who else could it have been? No servant would dare to commit such an act without express orders from the master. And surely Lord Vansittart would not trust to one of the maids to do his dirty work.

Cold and hunger alike forgotten, Isolde began once more to pace, prey to the certainty that Lord Vansittart intended her no good by this.

Had all the amity been false? He could never have meant to offer her a home. Then what did he intend? He did not trust her, that was plain. Did he imagine she would raid the house in the night and make off with the silver or some such thing? Not that Isolde supposed there was anything of great value in the place. If she'd realised nothing else, she could hardly fail to notice the clear lack of funds. Else he would not have allowed his house to fall into such disrepair.

But it made no sense. She'd made it clear to him she had nowhere to go. He could not seriously suppose she might abscond. Then what did he mean by this?

She could find no satisfactory answer. His welcome must have been a lie. Yet if he did not want her, why should he make it impossible for her to leave?

There was only one sure conclusion to be drawn. Lord Vansittart was up to no good. Her instinct had led her to distrust him and she'd been right.

In a bang, she remembered Richard's words. Vansittart was trying to ruin him!

Isolde felt as if the cold of the morning had entered her veins. He meant mischief all right, but not against her. He was plotting to use her in his battle with Richard.

Sudden dread speared the unacknowledged hope Isolde had not allowed herself to feel. Now, it was less a thing of hope than a certainty.

How could she have been so stupid? Of course Richard would follow her! The moment he knew how Alicia had treated her, he would come after her. After the last farewell before he went to London, Isolde could have no doubt he would not rest until he found her.

She had made it horribly easy. Wouldn't he guess at once that she would try Vansittart first?

Her heartbeat quickened. Richard was walking straight into a trap.

Chapter Twenty

Richard woke to the conviction that something was wrong. He lay in the darkness of the curtained bed, blinking away sleep and trying to focus his mind. Was it a bad dream? He groped for a memory and found none.

Some alien sound must have woken him. Where was he? Oh yes, The Cock at Bishop's Stortford. His late arrival had discomposed the hosts, causing a degree of chaos as a room was hastily prepared and a kitchen minion sent to rustle up some leftovers by way of a meal. Richard had made sure of his groom's comfort as well as his own, and had dispensed largesse among the stable hands, for the horses were all but spent and in need of rubbing dry and warming before being bedded down for the night. The last few miles through gathering snow had been a severe trial on all of them, and Richard had very nearly abandoned his purpose to seek shelter at the nearest inn.

Now he was glad he'd pushed on to reach his objective, for he was situated but a mile or two from Vansittart's house and the weather could not delay him. A sense of urgency crept over him, although he could not put a name to the apprehension that steadily increased as the moments ticked by.

Alert now, he flung off the covers, whisked the curtain back and sought under the pillow for his pocket watch.

Six and thirty? With an exasperated sigh, he dropped back onto the pillows. A ridiculous time to be awake. The inn must be stirring, but it was far too early to be up and about. He could be off within the hour, but it was futile to suppose Vansittart's household would be all alive and ready to receive a visitor. Assuming Isolde was there, she would be still abed. As

166

for the fellow himself, he was scarcely the type of man to rise with the lark.

Yet the feeling of wrongness persisted. Richard was beset with a reckless desire to throw caution to the winds and follow his instinct. He forced himself to think it through.

What possible danger could there be? He knew Vansittart for a schemer, but he did not take him for an out and out villain. He might repudiate his niece. He would not harm her.

It struck him then and Richard smote his own forehead. How could he be so dull-witted?

Vansittart had always an eye to the main chance. The man would think first and foremost about how Isolde could be useful to him. A bargaining chip.

Richard cursed. Had he not thought just the same himself?

The notion was scarcely formed before he was out of bed and reaching for the bell, a chaos of discomforting images flying through his head. Unformed, vague and incoherent, they took a common theme. Isolde in trouble.

It was a full minute before Isolde remembered her cloak and the pistol reposing in the pocket.

Cursing herself, she hunted about for where she'd put the thing. She could have been warmer all this time. Had she thrown it down somewhere? Her eyes had become accustomed to the gloom, but still she could not see it. Or was it growing lighter?

Crossing to the window, she found the world outside was glimmering, a sheen of white everywhere. Disoriented, Isolde stared harder. The oddness found shape. It had snowed in the night. No wonder the atmosphere was so still and cold.

Leaning into the glass, she squinted down. Difficult to see what lay below the window. Grasping the handles, she flung up the lower half of the sash window, gasping at the rush of icy air that burned her cheeks and caught in her throat. Leaning out, she looked down.

Dark shapes lurked dimly in the shadows beneath. Isolde could not judge the distance to the ground, and no convenient tree or climbing plant offered succour for a fugitive bent upon removing from this room. No escape by way of the window then.

She pulled back in and slammed it shut, not without a feeling of relief. The thought of scrabbling down the wall in the gloom was not a welcome one.

The blast of cold had left the chamber even icier than before. Shivering, Isolde turned from the window and something between the open bed-curtains caught her eye. A vague memory formed. Half asleep in one of her waking times she'd dragged the cloak over the bedclothes for extra warmth.

With a cry of triumph, she rushed to retrieve it, fumbling for the heavy weight in the pocket with trembling fingers.

The cold steel of the pistol in her hands, her heart began to thump with a mixture of excitement and dread. She dared not check the pan, for fear of losing the ball. She could only hope the powder had not become damp in the cold.

Setting the pistol down with care, she donned the cloak. The thick wool had an instant effect and her taut breath calmed a little. Grasping the weapon, she approached the door and aimed the muzzle at her target, standing well back.

Cocking the gun, Isolde drew a breath, and fired.

The explosion shattered the silence and the door jumped free as the lock splintered.

Isolde staggered a little from the recoil but she wasted no time. The household would be about her in a trice.

She was through the door in a twinkling, speeding down the corridor. There was no point in keeping quiet now, and her footsteps pounded as she hit the stairs. Grabbing the rail for support, she ran down and made for the front door.

Shouts echoed around the house as she struggled to reach a fat bolt at the top of the door. Footsteps were approaching. In her frantic ears, they sounded as if they were coming from every direction.

"Hold! You there, stop!"

Isolde turned her head. A burly fellow in livery was behind her. She raised the pistol.

"Stand off from me or I will shoot you down!"

The footman backed away in a hurry. Isolde held the gun on him, her mind working. Could she manage the bolts and keep him covered? Even if she got out, she still had to find her way to the stables and saddle the horse. Escape seemed impossible, but she had to try.

She shifted back from the door and waved her free hand at the footman.

"Open it!"

He moved with alacrity, one eye on the pistol in her hand. As he tugged on the bolt that had defeated Isolde, an irate voice spoke from the gallery above.

"Leave it, you fool! She's fired the gun. It's no longer loaded."

Isolde wheeled about. Her uncle, clad in a nightshirt with a gown flung haphazardly over it, was leaning across the bannister on the landing. Her temper broke.

"You fiend! How dared you lock me in? What did you intend?"

He ignored her, instead gesturing to the footman. "Lay hold on her, Jarvis!"

Even as the fellow seized her, he looked with puzzled gaze from Isolde to his master. "Her, my lord? But —"

"It's a female in disguise. Use your eyes, for God's sake!"

Furious, Isolde struggled to free herself. "Take your hands off me!"

"Get the pistol from her."

The command was uttered with calm, but Isolde was not similarly quiet. She fought to keep hold of the gun, but she was no match for the footman who wrested it from her.

Chagrined, she turned back to confront her uncle and discovered he was now flanked by the maid she'd met yesterday. The girl was still in her nightgown and Isolde drew an instant conclusion. Schooled by her father's association with Mrs Quick, she guessed the maid was keeping her uncle's bed warm.

"Aggy, take this," the footman called out before Isolde could speak.

Looking round she saw the young chambermaid come forward from where she stood before the servants' door. She took the pistol gingerly, holding it between thumb and forefinger away from her body, as if it had the power to attack her.

A riffle of relief went through Isolde. She had a much better chance of getting the pistol away from the maid than from the footman.

"Take her away and keep her secure in the scullery."

The sound of Lord Vansittart's languid voice, as much as his words, threw Isolde into rebellion. Resisting the footman's efforts to pull her in the direction of the green baize door, she hurled defiance at her uncle.

"You won't get away with this, my lord Vansittart. I know what you would be at and it won't work. You mean to use me to make mischief with Richard."

"Mischief? No indeed, my dear. I am merely taking advantage of a tool that came to my hand."

"Yes, for you mean to ruin him."

A light laugh floated down the stairway. "Is that what the estimable Richard told you? Dear me. I fear he overrates my powers."

"He knows you for what you are, and so do I. You won't best him."

"I don't need to. I have only to hold you, and wait. Take her away."

Isolde pulled back, kicking out at the man who was trying to drag her away.

"No! Let me go," she yelled again, desperate to make an impression. "You think he'll come here, but he won't. He doesn't even know I've left Bawdsey Grange."

"Hold!"

The footman paused and Isolde breathed more easily for the respite as she watched her uncle descend the stairs in a leisurely way. His gaze was fixed upon hers as he came towards her.

"You show pluck, I'll give you that, Isolde."

"Don't call me by my name!"

He gave this no attention. "Tell me, what makes you so sure Alderton will not come for you?"

Isolde glared at him. "Yes, you thought you could use me as bait, did you not? I came to you for succour and you pretended to offer me a home only so that you might take advantage."

"All very true, but that does not answer my question."

Isolde thought fast. "In the first place, Richard is in London. He is not expected back for days."

"Indeed?"

She did not like the mocking smile glimmering in her uncle's face. Striving for as sneering a tone as his own, she pursued her purpose. "Even if he did think to follow me when he comes back, he has no idea where I've gone. He doesn't even know I'm related to you."

The moment the lie was out of her mouth, she knew she'd made a mistake. Triumph glittered in Lord Vansittart's eyes, so dismayingly a mirror of her own.

"I can't make up my mind which of you is the greater fool, you or Alderton. Had he told you of his visit here, no doubt you would have known better than to try to pull the wool over my eyes, my dear."

Isolde's pulses quickened. "Richard came here? You said he never spoke to you."

"I said he did not write to me about you. How little you know of the man, my poor dear Isolde. He is far too righteous for his own good. He played his hand too well. I believe he expressly stated that nothing would induce him to abandon you to my tender mercies. So you see, my dear, I am far better acquainted with his probable actions than are you."

Isolde gazed at him appalled, yet prey to a sputter of hot feeling that threatened a prickle at her eyes and a thickening in her throat. Richard had cared enough, even then, to wish to protect her from her uncle.

His peculiarly mocking smile reappeared. "Dear me, I appear to have taken your breath away. I do trust you will not suffer too many pangs of remorse for presenting yourself here, like a lamb to the slaughter."

She did not trust herself to speak, closing her lips upon the futile words of heated recrimination that rose to her tongue.

He laughed gently. "I shall go and dress. It would not do to be taken unawares. Jarvis, you have your orders."

Isolde made no resistance this time as she was hauled off towards the nether regions, beset as she was by too many conflicting emotions to have the strength to fight back.

On tenterhooks, Isolde tried to thrust down the rising panic and work out a plan. Who knew how long it might take Richard to catch up with her? The one grain of truth in the story she'd used to try to fob off her uncle was that she had no notion when Richard planned his return from London. The only certain thing was that he would not be long delayed, with Christmas right around the corner. She might be held here for days, which must at least afford her an opportunity to get away. She began to hope Richard would indeed be held up, giving her longer for a way to evade her uncle. She was not a soldier's daughter for nothing. Her pistol had been confiscated, but she still had her sword. Unless it had been discovered when the groom unsaddled the mare?

It would be politic to retrieve the pistol if she could. She had ball and shot in her saddlebags. Unfortunately, the footman had possessed himself of the gun, taking it away from Aggy and sending the girl about her business. It was a setback, but perhaps not altogether impossible.

Glancing sideways at the fellow Jarvis, she weighed her chances at deception. He had been persuaded easily enough to allow her to remove to the kitchen. Likely he had no wish to remain in the cold scullery himself, when a welcome fire beckoned. Isolde had seated herself at the kitchen table, deliberately cultivating a pose of dejection, as if she was defeated.

The cook was busy at the oven in the wall, from which emanated the aroma of fresh-baked bread. Isolde's hunger revived. She adopted a conciliatory tone. "Do you think I could have something to eat?"

The cook looked round. The footman glanced up from his position to one side where he leaned against the wall, hefting the gun from hand to hand.

"Suppose there's no harm in that." He nodded to the cook. "Give her one of them rolls."

The woman scowled. "They ain't ready."

"Make her something then."

"Haven't I got enough to do as it is, getting the master's breakfast?"

Jarvis clicked his tongue. "Just do it."

Grumbling, the cook set a flat pan on the stove and ambled over to her cupboards. Isolde watched her hover over a bowl of eggs and her mouth watered.

If the footman was well enough disposed to procure her a portion of breakfast, perhaps he might be amenable to reason.

"Would you let me have my pistol back?"

Jarvis let out a rude crack of laughter. "You must be off your head, miss. The master would have mine if I did."

"But even he knew it was no longer a danger to anyone. I can't reload it."

"Then what d'you want it for?"

Isolde schooled her features to what she hoped was an expression of sadness and put a plea in her voice. "You see, it belonged to my papa, and he died. I would hate to lose it."

The footman looked at the pistol in his hand and back to Isolde. Then he shrugged.

"Why should I trouble my head about it? Dare say the master will take it from you if he wants. Here."

He held it out, and Isolde took it with a word of thanks and a heart teeming with triumph. She tucked it into the pocket of her cloak before he could change his mind.

The cook's bulk intervened between him and Isolde as she laid down a tankard with a plonk. "You can drink this, if you like."

Isolde gave her a smile. "Thank you."

She picked up the tankard and looked inside. Was it ale? She took a cautious sip. A tang of citrus snaked into her nostrils and a sweet, cloying taste hit the back of her throat and turned unexpectedly hot. Isolde coughed and set the drink down, looking at the cook's back where she was now busy with a skillet in the pan on the stove.

"What is this?"

"Ginger tea." The woman glanced over her shoulder. "It'll warm you up."

Isolde was touched. The cook was more sympathetic than she had supposed. Taking another sip, she took care to suck it back to mitigate the shock of heat. The liquid slid down and she felt it all the way to her stomach.

For a few minutes she sipped in silence. By the time the cook set a plate of scrambled eggs before her, she was feeling decidedly warmer and her nerves began to settle.

She had just lifted a forkful of food to her mouth when a sound from outside that had been hovering in the background of her mind abruptly took shape. She glanced at the footman, who, from his stance, had clearly heard it too.

"Is that horses?"

They were muffled, but it was certainly the sound of hooves. Jarvis did not answer, only crossing to the back window and looking out.

Just then a bell pealed through the hallway beyond the kitchen and the footman's head jerked round. "That's the front door, that is."

Isolde's heart jerked. Richard! Could it be? It seemed unlikely so early.

The footman brushed past the cook, throwing a command over his shoulder on his way to the door. "Watch her!"

Waiting only for the fellow to leave the room, Isolde leaped from her chair and ran to the back window.

"Hoy!"

She turned quickly to find the cook lumbering in her direction.

"It's all right. I'm not going anywhere. I just want to see who it is."

She peered out, aware of the woman coming up behind her.

The day was considerably lightened by this time, and the snow out the back was criss-crossed with patterns of footsteps. The hoofbeats were slow, but coming closer. As she watched, a curricle rounded the corner and headed towards a block of buildings some little distance from the back of house. Was it the stables?

Her breath had misted the glass and Isolde brought up her arm, brushing at the window with her sleeve. As the image cleared, she saw the equipage more clearly and recognised the face of the groom who was driving the team. She'd seen him at Bawdsey Grange. Her pulse skittered. Then Richard was here!

Imperative to get out of this kitchen. She must talk to the groom. Get to the stables if she could and retrieve her sword.

When she turned, she found the cook in her way. The woman nodded towards the window.

"Know him?"

Careful now. Subterfuge was necessary. Isolde shrugged. "I have no idea who he is."

She shifted around the cook's body and made for the table, while surreptitiously glancing across to the back door and judging the distance. She'd need to be quick.

She sat down and took up her fork again, waiting for the woman to return to her cooking pots. The instant her back was turned, Isolde rose, picked up her plate and threw it across the room towards the inner door.

The woman cried out and turned towards the sound. Isolde bolted for the back door, dragged it open and fled into the snow.

Chapter Twenty-one

"His lordship is not yet up, sir."

Richard eyed the footman. Was there a shifty look about him? The fellow could not meet his gaze and slid a glance up towards the stairs. Watching for his master?

"Go and tell him Lord Alderton is here and wishes to see him immediately."

The footman hesitated. "I don't think his lordship —"

"Enough. Fetch him down!"

The sharp tone had an effect as the man visibly blenched. Remembering where he had been received before, Richard moved to the door on the right.

"I'll wait in here."

The footman hurried to open the door for him and bowed him in. "As your lordship pleases."

Richard marched into the room, still clad in his outer garments. He took off his hat and threw it on the nearest chair as he passed, pacing. Something was up. He felt it in the footman's attitude, in the unnatural quiet of the house. His instinct had not led him astray. Anxiety built again, his head full of Isolde.

At least he was here, on the spot. Whatever had occurred, he could act swiftly.

Moments passed. They felt like hours. If Vansittart was abed, it could take a while for him to dress. But the apparent calm of his household was spurious. At this hour, servants should be busy preparing for the day. Part of Richard wanted to bypass all common sense and set up a search of the house. But that would be futile. If the fellow had Isolde stashed somewhere, she could be in any of the rooms.

Before he could work himself into a lather of worry, the door opened and Vansittart walked in. To Richard's irritation, he looked as point de vice as ever, in grey breeches and a salmon coat. His manner was suave to the point of insulting.

"You choose an early hour to pay morning calls, Alderton."

Richard wasted no time. "Where is Isolde?"

The pale brows rose. "My niece? But, my dear Alderton, she was surely in your charge, was she not?"

With difficulty, Richard suppressed the desire to drive his fist into that complacent face. "Don't play games with me, Vansittart. I know she's here."

"And how do you come by such certainty?"

"Deduction. And my knowledge of her. She lost her home with me in my absence, and came to you, as she had intended to do in due course."

Vansittart's mocking smile appeared. "Admirable, my dear fellow. No doubt you are also able to foresee my reaction?"

Richard almost snorted. "With ease. You don't want her, but you hope to use her to force my hand."

"I make you my compliments, Alderton. Your intelligence is like to save us a deal of time." He moved in his leisurely way towards the two chairs by the fireplace, where their earlier discussion had taken place. "Come, let us be comfortable while we negotiate."

Richard stood his ground. "There will be no negotiation. I repeat, where is Isolde?"

"Oh, safe enough, I assure you. I wish you will sit down."

"I do not stir until I have had a sight of her. I trust you as little as I would a snake. Until I know she has received no sort of hurt at your hands, I have nothing to say."

He looked to see how the other took this, and found him smiling with the smug expression Richard itched to spoil. But a turn-up would not help them. He resisted the urge to demand Isolde once again, and waited.

After a moment, Vansittart went to the bell-pull and tugged. As if he had been waiting outside, the footman appeared through the door, but his words belied the impression.

"He's gone, my lord! I mean, she's gone. She gave us the slip."

The change in Vansittart was startling. Thunder leapt to his face and his eyes flared.

"Fools! Idiots! Where the devil is she then?"

A voice in his rear spoke up. "I am here, Uncle."

The man turned sharply and Richard's heart kicked. Across the room stood Isolde, sword in hand. In seconds she was at full lunge, the point inches from Vansittart's chest.

"Do not move, or I will spit you where you stand."

The room froze. Richard saw momentary terror in Vansittart's face. It was veiled swiftly. To his credit, the man achieved a semblance of his normal drawl.

"Is this your influence, Alderton? What in the world have you been teaching the chit?"

A faint laugh escaped Richard despite his inner tension. "It has nothing to do with me. This is who Isolde is."

There was time for no more. Isolde pulled back to the on guard position, but the menace remained in both stance and voice.

"You won't use me against Richard. I won't let you. I'll die first."

"Tut, so fierce, my dear? Put up your sword, I beg of you. There is no need for violence."

"Yes, there is. Every need. I never wanted to come to you and I see I was right. You are an evil man and my mother was well rid of you and your foul family."

Richard heard the upset under the venom and a dart pierced him. The child had been hurt in more ways than one. He judged it time to intervene. "Isolde!"

An error, as he saw at once. Her eyes turned towards him. The split second off guard was enough. The footman pounced. The impact took Isolde at the shoulder and bore her to the ground.

Richard moved, but he was not fast enough. The struggle lasted but seconds. Before he well knew what had happened, Vansittart was in possession of the sword, the footman was struggling with a kicking and screaming Isolde and a third man, appearing suddenly among them, added a hoarse shout to the mêlée.

"Behind you, my lord!"

Recognizing Reeve's voice, Richard turned fast and found himself confronted by a maid wielding a warming pan. With instant presence of mind, he batted the thing away and it flew from the maid's hands. The clatter as it landed added to the cacophony.

"Help Miss Cavanagh!" Richard shouted, grappling with the maid, who had attacked without her weapon, throwing her weight into his chest and battering at him with curled fists.

His attention on how Isolde was faring put Richard out of kilter and he was aware he was not operating as sensibly as he should. He pulled himself together, seized the maid's wrists and manhandled her to the door, which was open. He hurled her into the hall, where she fell and slid across the floor.

Without pausing to see where she landed, Richard slammed the door and raced to the grunting battle in the middle of the room. The sword was nowhere to be seen and his groom was wrestling with Vansittart, whose appearance was now considerably the worse for wear. A momentary satisfaction did not vanquish Richard's wits.

Rather than enter the fray, he extracted his pistol from his pocket and levelled it at Vansittart. "Reeve, desist! Let him go. Help Miss Cavanagh."

Released, Vansittart swung towards Richard with fists raised to strike. He met the muzzle of the gun as Richard shoved it into his chest.

"I wouldn't, if I were you. This pistol is cocked and it has a hair trigger."

Vansittart was already still, his eyes on the weapon. He shifted a step back, from somewhere dragging up the remnants of his habitual manner.

"Well, well, perhaps I should no longer wonder at Isolde's tricks. You appear to be two of a kind."

Richard paid no heed. Without taking his eyes off Vansittart, he addressed the groom. "Is she safe?"

The noise of struggles had ceased. He could hear panting and grunts.

"Got him, my lord. She's safe enough, but still on the floor."

Richard did not dare look, though every instinct screamed at him to check. He called out instead: "Isolde, can you stand?"

"I think so."

Her voice was faint, and he felt his stomach tighten. She was hurt. Fury swamped him. "By heaven, Vansittart, I am minded to dispose of you out of hand!"

The other man raised placatory hands. "Not so fast. I feel sure we can make our way through this."

"Call off your tool. Send him away."

For a moment, the fellow hesitated. Evidently feeling himself outfoxed, he capitulated, to Richard's secret relief.

"Go, Jarvis."

The footman was assisted on his way by the toe of the groom's boot.

"Here, Reeve, take my pistol and cover his lordship. If he moves, shoot him."

"It'd be a pleasure, my lord."

The groom in his place, Richard went quickly to Isolde. She had struggled to a sitting position, but she had a hand to her head.

"Come." With gentleness, Richard took her by the arms and helped her to stand. "Are you hurt?"

"Bruised, I think. A bit dazed."

"We'll have you comfortable in a trice. Let me deal with your uncle and we'll be away."

She nodded and he guided her with an arm about her shoulders, holding her close and steady against him. Together, they faced Vansittart.

"Pay close attention, my friend, and you will learn how this is going to go."

Chapter Twenty-two

Isolde polished off the last slice of ham, took another swallow of coffee and sat back with a satisfied sigh. She found Richard watching her from across the table, a faint smile curling his mouth. She grinned. "I was starving."

"Yes, so I gathered."

His gaze did not waver and Isolde began to fidget, turning the coffee cup in her hands. A pitter-patter disturbed her heartbeat and she shifted her eyes about the tiny parlour, hardly taking in the dark wood panelling and the leaded window. In her mind's eye, the events of the morning played out in snatches of unfocused memory.

Her uncle's face, marred by a heavy frown, and words on his lips that made no sense. "A settlement? What sort of settlement?"

Then Richard's dry tones. "I should have thought that was obvious."

Lord Vansittart's eyes had turned on her and Isolde remembered shrinking closer to Richard's side as the mockery reappeared in her uncle's voice.

"That scrap? Are you serious?"

"Perfectly."

Her focus returned now to Richard's face. "What settlement were you discussing with my uncle earlier?"

His gaze remained steady on hers. "I made a bargain with him."

Apprehension warred with dawning fury. "You're not letting him bleed you? You can't, Richard! He's a villain. Please don't give him anything."

His regard faltered for the first time, flitting away and back again. Isolde's burgeoning anger gave way to puzzlement. She'd never seen him lose his assurance, but there was uncertainty, was there not?

"Richard?"

He visibly drew breath. "I am going to pay him a certain sum of money." He held up a finger as Isolde opened her mouth to protest. "Not for his vile schemes. I told him I will not invest one penny to support slavery."

"Slavery?"

"He has bought into a cotton plantation in America. He tried to engage my father's interest in taking a share in this business. Only I found out he means to purchase slaves to work these cotton fields."

Her fury revived. "I told you he is a villain. Don't give him money, Richard. He'll use it for that anyway."

"No. My lawyer will ensure the settlement is tied. It won't be a blank draft for him to do with as he wills."

"But why pay him anything? He can't use me now to force your hand."

"Ah, but I have extracted a valuable exchange."

Isolde stared at him, bewildered. "What? What could possibly be worth giving my horrid uncle anything at all?"

Again, Richard hesitated. He rose from the table and walked the short few paces to the mantel in the little room. There had barely been space for Isolde to squeeze into her seat. As she watched him, a sixth sense attacked her with a gust of shocked hope. He could not mean…

Her mind balked. Her breath caught and she could not speak. In mingled dread and anticipation, she saw him turn his head, an expression she did not recognise in his eyes. Only their intensity penetrated.

"You, Isolde. I get you."

Her voice stuck in her throat and the wild thump of her heart sounded loud in her ears. Thoughts filtered into her clogged mind. She dared not give them house room. Too dangerous. If she were wrong, if she'd misunderstood…

There was no air in the room. Heat crept up from her toes, spreading through her veins, sending a wash of flame into her cheeks. From nowhere, she found words.

"But you don't even like me."

He threw back his head and let out a crack of a laugh. "Whatever gave you that idea?"

Now words tumbled, eager to come out. "You've been kind, but you know very well you never wanted the charge of me. And then Lady Alderton died and everything was horrid between us…"

Richard's eyes were dark with feeling to which she could not put a name, but he did not move from where he stood. "I hurt you, and I'm sorry for it. But not nearly as sorry as I am that I left you to Alicia's vengeance. I had no idea of her state of mind. I am ashamed that you were subjected to such brutality, that you were treated in so inhuman a fashion in my house."

Isolde's heart sank. Was that why? Then she must have misunderstood him. He could only be thinking of making some sort of reparation. She found her tongue again.

"You will remain my guardian then? Is that what you mean? Why should you need to make an exchange with my uncle for that?"

He let go the mantel and took a step towards the table, a frown creasing his brow.

"It has some value. In return, he will acknowledge you in public, which will give you credit with Society and make your path easier. But I'm not going to remain your guardian, Isolde."

Dismay flooded her, and she had to drop her eyes to hide the sudden rush of tears. She was aware of him watching her and struggled to find her voice. But what came out of her mouth was not at all what she'd meant to say. "I knew you didn't want me."

"Then you know nothing at all," came the harsh response. "I want you more than I can describe."

When the sense of this penetrated, she gasped with shock, looking up to find his eyes fixed upon hers. Then she was on her feet. "Richard, it won't work. I'm all wrong. I was foisted on you. You need a — a proper lady."

He moved. Her hand was seized and she stumbled out from behind the table. Next moment, strong arms held her. She could feel his heart pumping as hard as her own. She could not look away from the intense dark gaze boring down into hers.

"You are all the lady I need, Isolde. I think I felt it from the first moment of setting eyes on you. I fooled myself into believing it was not so, that what I felt for you was only sympathy. But when I saw you stand up so bravely to Vansittart, I could no longer deceive myself."

She could not help it. The prick at her throat became a swelling and a sob burst out. His face changed.

"What is it? Am I wrong? I could have sworn — the way you looked at me… Isolde, don't you want to marry me?"

Tears spilled down her cheeks and her voice came out a croak. "Yes. Oh yes, I do. So much!"

He dragged her tighter and his lips came down on hers. Isolde went weak, the featherlight touch a burn on her mouth.

A noise in the corridor made him release her, and she staggered on unruly knees. Uttering an oath, he moved swiftly to the door and turned the key in the lock. His smile was rueful as he returned to claim her and pull her back into his arms, where she settled with relief, glad of his strength in keeping her on her unsteady feet.

"The last thing we need is for a servant to see me kissing you while you are wearing that get-up."

Isolde giggled. "We'll start a shocking scandal."

"Yes, just exactly what we need to avoid."

His face came down. He was going to kiss her again. She closed her eyes, melting against him. The burn became a flame and her mind ceased to function, her veins running riot with feeling. When his mouth released hers, she opened them to find his dark eyes studying hers, looking from one to the other, a faint frown between his brows.

"I can't make up my mind."

She blinked. "What?"

"Your eyes. Are they green with gold flecks, or hazel with patches of green?"

"I have no notion."

He sighed deeply. "Oh, Isolde, I'm so horribly in love with you."

"Horribly?" Indignation rose in her breast and she tugged herself out of his arms. "There now, I told you I was all wrong."

He made no attempt to recapture her, but his gaze roved her features, tenderness in his face. "No, you're not. You're everything I've ever wanted, though indeed I did not understand it myself until today."

"Richard, you've run mad."

"Yes, but I don't regret it for a moment."

Agitation claimed her and she shifted away. "But you may."

"Never."

He made to seize her and she held her hands up to stop him. "No, don't. Please listen."

He dropped back, a frown replacing the smile. "Go on."

She drew a taut breath. "It's all very well for you to say these things, but all I've learned is only on the surface. I'll never really be a lady, you know I won't. Besides, if you marry me, Alicia will have won. She thinks I've been scheming to ensnare you all this time, only I never dared — never supposed —"

"No, you didn't. You are too much an innocent."

"Not so innocent I did not realise I was falling in love with you, though I tried so hard to pretend otherwise. So quickly, Richard! How is it possible?"

"Don't ask me. I'm as bemused as you, though I strongly suspect my mother guessed from the first where my inclination was leading me."

"And mine, I think. But — I'm sorry to pain you, Richard, in saying this — but she's gone. Your sister —"

"My darling girl, you need not give Alicia another thought."

"She hates me. She'll call me names and beat me. She'll never let me marry you."

Richard caught at her waving hands. "She'll have no chance to stop it. I will procure a licence and we may be married before we go back, if you are willing."

Isolde's heart soared. "Willing? I'd marry you tomorrow if it was possible. But I'm under age, Richard!"

"That need not trouble us."

"I won't have you ask my horrid uncle for permission."

He grinned as he drew her towards him. "No need. I'm your official guardian, remember? I have a letter to that effect. And I give myself full permission to marry you."

She sighed with happiness and began to sink into his embrace when a horrid thought assailed her, and she pulled back. "But, Richard, no priest will marry us with me dressed like this. It would be too scandalous."

His eyes were alight with laughter. "I'd give a great deal to try it, but you need not concern yourself. Becky packed your female attire. We'll find a small unobtrusive inn somewhere on the road and smuggle you in to change."

She could not help giggling. "That will be an adventure in itself."

He caressed her face, smiling down at her. "I should have thought you'd had enough adventure to last you for some little time."

In a bang, Isolde recalled the hideous events that had set her upon this journey, and the nagging apprehension revived. "Alicia —"

"Need never trouble you, my heart. I know what she did to you, for the servants told me. Becky was particularly informative."

She eyed him in dismay, hating the notion that he knew what she had suffered. She would not willingly have told him all of it herself. "What did she tell you?"

"Everything." He touched his finger to her cheek where she knew there were still remnants of her bruises. "My sister will never put a hand on you again, I promise you."

"How can you be so sure? You won't always be there to see it."

His face changed and the dismaying look of which she'd once been the target was back. She drew a breath, relieved his undeniable anger was not this time directed at her.

"It is Alicia who will not be there. I'm going to send her to the Dower House. You will be the only mistress at Bawdsey Grange."

The implication took a moment to penetrate, and shock put all thought of his fury with his sister out of her head. She stared at him aghast. "Richard, I can't! I don't know how."

His brows drew together. "You look positively petrified, Isolde."

"I am petrified!"

Richard's expression changed abruptly and his laugh produced a touch of reassurance. Her fears began to abate.

"You need have no apprehension. Mrs Pennyfather won't need your help, and she will teach you everything you need to know. As for the rest —"

Isolde pounced on this. "Yes, what of the rest, Richard? Who is going to make a lady of me?"

"I will. Enough of a lady to pass muster in public, at any rate." His lips twitched, in the way she remembered from the first. "But for myself, I've conceived a violent dislike of proper ladies."

She broke into laughter. "You're making that up."

He caught her face between his hands, and her breath tightened as a look she could not mistake crept into his eyes. His voice dropped to a murmur. "Your smile is like a sunbeam. I believe it captured my heart on the day we met." Then he was smiling with her and her heart turned over. "And no, my precious Isolde, I'm not making it up. I am quite decided. I have no use for a proper lady. I need only the unique, indomitable little creature who was ready to fight for me against all odds."

Isolde heaved a huge sigh of satisfaction, allowed herself to be drawn back into his welcoming arms and, hazy with the effect of his kiss, resolved with considerable relief to abandon her futile attempts to master the intricacies of ladylike behaviour.

A NOTE TO THE READER

Dear Reader,

In this world where women juggle careers and motherhood, rule countries or police forces and play professional football, it is hard for us to imagine how restrictive life was for the Regency female.

Difficult enough if you were born to domestic servitude or some other menial labouring capacity. Tricky if you rose to the middle classes where at once a woman's choices of workplace became fewer. In many ways, however, the least enviable strata was that of genteel poverty.

A female of gentle birth relied wholly on her menfolk for support. To have any security at all, her first object must be marriage. What happened to those who failed to find a husband? A dowerless female, for example. Women were expected to bring something concrete to the marriage in terms of finance or property. If you were lucky, your father or brother had the means to keep you in relative comfort all your life, although you could expect to be palmed off on a sibling for the purpose of helping to take care of the children.

Not all Regency females had this advantage. Orphans and poor relations might hope for succour from their wider family. Assuming willingness on the part of said family. What if you had no one and were obliged to earn your living? There were only two acceptable professions: governess or schoolteacher and companion. Anything else took you so far outside your social sphere that there was no way back. Any form of trade was unthinkable.

The plight of such women has always intrigued me. Romance allows me to pluck them from their humdrum existence and alter their destiny to encompass love and happiness, just as with the fairy tale Cinderella. Such are the heroines of my Brides by Chance series. Like Isolde, they begin without hope of a happy ending and, through accident, adventure or sheer luck, their life is forever changed. Of course I plunge them into heartache first! Love has to come with a cost, no?

I hope you have enjoyed Isolde's story and it has inspired you to look out for more tales of my brides by chance.

If you would consider leaving a review, it would be much appreciated and very helpful. Do feel free to contact me on **elizabeth@elizabethbailey.co.uk**

or find me on **Facebook**, **Twitter**, **Goodreads** or my website **www.elizabethbailey.co.uk**.

Elizabeth Bailey

Sapere Books is an exciting new publisher of brilliant fiction and popular history.

To find out more about our latest releases and our monthly bargain books visit our website: **saperebooks.com**

Printed in Great Britain
by Amazon